This isn't real.

It wasn't real, but it felt real. It even looked real.

Diana was dressed in a strapless chiffon gown, midnight blue, with a dangerously low, plunging neckline. A glittering stone rested between her breasts. A sapphire. The sapphire necklace from the photo shoot.

"Please stop staring." She turned and met his gaze. At last.

Franco's body hardened the instant his eyes fixed with hers. As exquisite as the sapphire around her neck was, it didn't hold a candle to the violet depths of those luminescent eyes. "You're lovely."

She stared at him coldly. "Save it for the cameras, would you? There's no one here. You can drop the act."

"It's not an act. You look beautiful." He swallowed. Hard. "That's quite a dress."

"Just stop it, would you? I know we're supposed to be madly in love with each other in public. But in private, can we keep things professional? Please?"

Something about the way she said *please* grabbed Franco by the throat and refused to let go.

Had he really been

ago?

Yes. He had.

DRAKE DIAMO shines as bright as the gems in their window!

Dear Reader,

Welcome back to the glittering world of Drake Diamonds! *It Started with a Diamond* is the third book in my debut series for Special Edition. I've had so much fun writing these books. It's been like having breakfast, lunch and dinner at Tiffany's every single day. Who wouldn't love that?

It Started with a Diamond is the story of Diana Drake, diamond heiress and world-class equestrian. After suffering a fall during a competition, Diana returns home to New York to take the helm of the marketing department of the family jewelry empire and mend her heart. But the new face of Drake Diamonds is dangerous, brooding polo player Franco Andrade, who seems to want nothing more than to get her back in the saddle.

I learned so much while writing this book, especially about polo, the sport of kings. While researching *It Started with a Diamond*, I even got to attend my very first polo match with a professional polo player who was kind enough to explain what I was seeing. But this book is about more than the sport. It's about having the courage to start over when life knocks you down. It's about love and loyalty. And diamonds, too, of course!

If you enjoy *It Started with a Diamond*, be sure to check out the first two books in this series, *His Ballerina Bride* and *The Princess Problem*.

As always, thank you for reading!

Best wishes,

Teri Wilson

It Started with a Diamond

Teri Wilson

HARLEQUIN®SPECIAL EDITION®

Recycling programs
for this product may
not exist in your area.

ISBN-13: 978-0-373-62360-0

It Started with a Diamond

Printed in U.S.A.

www.Harlequin.com

Teri Wilson is a novelist for Harlequin. She is the author of *Unleashing Mr. Darcy*, now a Hallmark Channel Original Movie. Teri is also a contributing writer at HelloGiggles.com, a lifestyle and entertainment website founded by Zooey Deschanel that is now part of the *People* magazine, *TIME* magazine and *Entertainment Weekly* family. Teri loves books, travel, animals and dancing every day. Visit Teri at www.teriwilson.net or on Twitter, @teriwilsonauthr.

Books by Teri Wilson

Harlequin Special Edition

Drake Diamonds

His Ballerina Bride
The Princess Problem

HQN Books

Unmasking Juliet
Unleashing Mr. Darcy

Visit the Author Profile page
at Harlequin.com for more titles.

For Brant Schafer, because naming a polo pony after me will guarantee you a book dedication.

And for Roe Valentine, my dear writing friend and other half of the Sisterhood of the Traveling Veuve Clicquot.

Chapter One

"It's hard to be a diamond in a rhinestone world."
—Dolly Parton

Diana Drake wasn't sure about much in her life at the moment, but one thing was crystal clear—she wanted to strangle her brother.

Not her older brother, Dalton. She couldn't really muster up any indignation as far as her elder sibling went, despite the fact that she was convinced he was at least partially responsible for her current predicament.

But Dalton got a free pass. For now.

She owed him.

For one thing, she'd been living rent free in his swanky Lenox Hill apartment for the past several months. For another, he was a prince now. A literal Prince Charming. As such, he wasn't even in New York anymore. He was somewhere on the French Riviera polishing his crown or sitting on a throne or doing whatever it was princes did all day long.

Dalton's absence meant that Diana's younger brother, Artem, was the only Drake around to take the full brunt of her frustration. Which was a tad problematic since he was her boss now.

Technically.

Sort of.

But Diana would just have to overlook that minor point. She'd held her tongue for as long as humanly possible.

"I can't do it anymore," she blurted as she marched into his massive office on the tenth floor of Drake Diamonds, the legendary jewelry store situated on the corner of 5th Avenue and 57th Street, right in the glittering center of Manhattan. The family business.

Diana might not have spent every waking hour of her life surrounded by diamonds and fancy blue boxes tied with white satin bows, as Dalton had. And she might not be the chief executive officer, like Artem. But the last time she checked, she was still a member of the family. She was a Drake, just like the rest of them.

So was it really necessary to suffer the humiliation of working as a salesperson in the most dreaded section of the store?

"Engagements? *Really?*" She crossed her arms and glared at Artem. It was still weird seeing him sitting behind what used to be their father's desk. Gaston Drake had been dead for a nearly a year, yet his presence loomed large.

Too large. It was almost suffocating.

"Good morning to you, too, Diana." Artem smoothed down his tie, which was the exact same hue as the store's trademark blue boxes. *Drake* blue.

Could he have the decency to look at least a little bit bothered by her outburst?

Apparently not.

She sighed. "I can't do it, Artem. I'll work anywhere in this building, except *there*." She waved a hand in the direction of the Engagements showroom down the hall.

He stared blithely at her, then made a big show of looking at his watch. "I see your point. It's been all of three hours. However have you lasted this long?"

"Three *torturous* hours." She let out another massive sigh. "Have you ever set foot in that place?"

"I'm the CEO, so, yes, I venture over there from time to time."

Right. Of course he had.

Still, she doubted he'd actually helped any engaged couples choose their wedding rings. At least, she hoped he hadn't, mainly because she wouldn't have wished such a fate on her worst enemy.

This morning she'd actually witnessed a grown man and woman speaking baby talk to each other. Her stomach churned just thinking about it now. Adults had no business speaking baby talk, not even to actual babies.

Her gaze shifted briefly to the bassinet in the corner of her brother's office. She still couldn't quite believe Artem was a dad now. A husband. It was kind of mind-boggling when she thought about it, especially considering what an abysmally poor role model their father had been in the family department.

Keep it professional.

She wouldn't get anywhere approaching Artem as a sibling. This conversation was about business, plain and simple. Removing herself from Engagements was the best thing Diana could do, not just for herself, but also for Drake Diamonds.

Only half an hour ago, she'd had to bite her tongue when a man asked for advice about choosing an engagement ring and she'd very nearly told him to spend his money on something more sensible than a huge diamond when the chances that he and his girlfriend would live happily ever after were slim to none. *If* she accepted his proposal, they only had about an eighty percent chance of making it down the aisle. Beyond that, their odds of staying married were about fifty-fifty. Even if they remained husband and wife until death did them part, could they reasonably expect to be happy? Was *anyone* happily married?

Diana's own mother had stuck faithfully by her husband's side after she found out he'd fathered a child with their housekeeper, even when she ended up raising the boy herself. Surely that didn't count as a happy marriage.

That boy was now a man and currently seated across the desk from Diana. She'd grown up alongside Artem and couldn't possibly love him more. He was her brother. Case closed.

Diana's problem wasn't with Artem. It was with her father and the concept of marriage as a whole. She didn't like what relationships did to people...

Especially what one had done to her mother.

Even if she'd grown up in a picture-perfect model family, Diana doubted she'd ever see spending three months' salary on an engagement ring as anything but utter foolishness.

It was a matter of logic, pure and simple. Of statistics. And statistics said that plunking down $40,000 for a two-carat Drake Diamonds solitaire was like throwing a giant wad of cash right into the Hudson River.

But she had no business saying such things out loud since she worked in Engagements, now, did she? She had no business saying such things, period. Drake Diamonds had supported her for her entire life.

So she'd bitten her tongue. Hard.

"I'm simply saying that my talents would be best put to use someplace else." *Anyplace* else.

"Would they now?" Artem narrowed his gaze at her. A hint of a smile tugged at the corner of his mouth, and she knew what was coming. "And what talents would those be, exactly?"

And there it was.

"Don't start." She had no desire to talk about her accident again. Or ever, for that matter. She'd moved on.

Artem held up his hands in a gesture of faux surrender. "I didn't say a word about your training. I'm simply pointing out that you have no work experience. Or college education, for that matter. I hate to say it, sis, but your options are limited."

She'd considered enrolling in classes at NYU, but didn't bother mentioning it. Her degree wasn't going to materialize overnight. *Unfortunately.* College had always been on her radar, but between training and competing, she hadn't found the time. Now she was a twenty-six-year-old without a single day of higher education under her belt.

If only she'd spent a little less time on the back of a horse for the past ten years and a few more hours in the classroom…

She cleared her throat. "Do I need to remind you that I own a third of this business? You and Dalton aren't the only Drakes around here, you know."

"No, but we're the only ones who've actually worked here before today." He glanced at his watch again, stood and buttoned his suit jacket. "Look, just stick it out for a while. Once you've learned the ropes, we'll try and find another role for you. Okay?"

Awhile.

Just how long was that, she wondered. A week? A month? A year? She desperately wanted to ask, but she didn't dare. She hated sounding whiny, and she *really* hated relying on the dreadful Drake name. But it just so happened that name was the only thing she had going for her at the moment.

Oh, how the mighty had fallen. Literally.

"Come on." Artem brushed past her. "We've got a photo shoot scheduled this afternoon in Engagements. I think you might find it rather interesting."

She was glad to be walking behind him so he couldn't see her massive eyeroll. "Please tell me it doesn't involve a wedding dress."

"Relax, sister dear. We're shooting cuff links. The photographer only wanted to use the Engagements showroom because it has the best view of Manhattan in the building."

It did have a lovely view, especially now that spring had arrived in New York in all its fragrant splendor. The air was filled with cherry blossoms, swirling like pink snow flurries. Diana had lost herself a time or two staring out at the verdant landscape of Central Park.

But those few blissful moments had come to a crashing end the moment she'd turned away from the showroom's floor-to-ceiling windows and remembered she was surrounded by diamonds. Wedding diamonds.

And here I am again.

She blinked against the dazzling assault of countless engagement rings sparkling beneath the sales floor lights and followed Artem to the corner of the room where the photographer was busy setting up a pair of tall light stands. A row of camera lenses in different sizes sat on top of one of glass jewelry cases.

Diana slid a velvet jeweler's pad beneath the lenses to protect the glass and busied herself rearranging things. Maybe if she somehow inserted herself into this whole photo-shoot process, she could avoid being a part of anyone's betrothal for an hour or two.

A girl can dream.

"Is our model here?" the photographer asked. "Because I'm ready, and we've only got about an hour left until sundown. I'd like to capture some of this nice view before it's too late."

Diana glanced out the window. The sky was already tinged pale violet, and the evening wind had picked up, scattering pink petals up and down 5th Avenue. The sun was just beginning to dip below the skyscrapers. It would be a gorgeous backdrop...

...if the model showed up.

Artem checked his watch again and frowned in the direction of the door. Diana took her time polishing the half-dozen pairs of Drake cuff links he'd pulled for the shoot. Anything to stretch out the minutes.

Just as she reached for the last pair, Artem let out a sigh of relief. "Ah, he's here."

Diana glanced up, took one look at the man stalking toward them and froze. Was she hallucinating? Had the blow to the head she'd taken months ago done more damage than the doctors had thought?

Nothing is wrong with you. You're fine. Everything *is fine.*

Everything didn't feel fine, though. Diana's whole world had come apart, and months later she still hadn't managed to put it back together. She was beginning to think she never would.

Because, deep down, she knew she wouldn't. She couldn't pick up the pieces, even if she tried. No one could.

Which was precisely why she was cutting her losses and starting over again. She'd simply build a new life for herself. A normal life. Quiet. Safe. It would take some getting used to, but she could do it.

People started over all the time, didn't they?

At least she had a job. An apartment. A family. There were worse things in the world than being a Drake.

She was making a fresh start. She was a jeweler now. Her past was ancient history.

Except for the nagging fact that a certain man from her past was walking toward her. Here, now, in the very real present.

Franco Andrade.

Not him. Just...no.

She needed to leave. Maybe she could just slink over to one of the sales counters and get back to her champagne-sipping brides and grooms to be. Selling engagement rings had never seemed as appealing as it did right this second.

She laid her polishing cloth on the counter, but before she could place the cuff links back inside their neat blue box, one of them slipped right through her fingers. She watched in horror as it bounced off the tip of Artem's shoe and rolled across the plush Drake-blue carpet, straight toward Franco's approaching form.

Diana sighed. This is what she got for complaining to Artem. Just because she was an heiress didn't mean she had to act like one. Being entitled wasn't an admirable quality. Besides, karma was a raging bitch. One who didn't waste any time, apparently.

Diana dropped to her knees and scrambled after the

runaway cuff link, wishing the floor would somehow open up and swallow her whole. Evidently, there were indeed fates worse than helping men choose engagement rings.

"Mr. Andrade, we meet at last." Artem deftly side-stepped her and extended a hand toward Franco.

Mr. Andrade.

So it *was* him. She'd still been holding out the tiniest bit of hope for a hallucination. Or possibly a doppelganger. But that was an absurd notion. Men as handsome as Franco Andrade didn't roam the Earth in pairs. His kind of chiseled bone structure was a rarity, something that only came around once in a blue moon. Like a unicorn. Or a fiery asteroid hurtling toward Earth, promising mass destruction on impact.

One of those two things. The second, if the rumors of his conquests were to be believed.

Who was she kidding? She didn't need to rely on rumors. She knew firsthand what kind of man Franco Andrade was. It was etched in her memory with excruciating clarity. What she didn't know was what he was doing here.

Was he the model for the new campaign? Impossible.

It had to be some kind of joke. Or possibly Artem's wholly inappropriate attempt to manipulate her back into her old life.

Either way, for the second time in a matter of hours, she wanted to strangle her brother. He was the one who'd invited Franco here, after all. Perhaps joining the family business hadn't been her most stellar idea.

As if she had any other options.

She pushed Artem's reminders of her inadequate education and employment record out of her head and concentrated on the mortifying matter at hand. Where was that darn cuff link, anyway?

"Gotcha," she whispered under her breath as she caught sight of a silver flash out of the corner of her eye.

But just as she reached for it, Franco Andrade's ridiculously masculine form crouched into view. "Allow me."

His words sent a tingle skittering through her. Had his voice always been so deliciously low? The man could recite the alphabet and bring women to their knees. Which would have made the fact that she was already in just such a position convenient, had it not been so utterly humiliating.

"Here." He held out his hand. The cuff link sat nestled in the center of his palm. He had large hands, rough with calluses, a stark contrast to the finely tailored fit of his custom tuxedo.

Of course that tuxedo happened to be missing a tie, and his shirt cuffs weren't even fastened. He looked as if he'd just rolled out of someone's bed and tossed on his discarded Armani from the night before.

Then again, he most likely had.

"Thank you," she mumbled, steadfastly refusing to meet his gaze.

"Wait." He balled his fist around the cuff link and stooped lower to peer at her. "Do we know each other?"

"Nope." She shook her head so hard she could practically hear her brain rattle. "No, I'm afraid we don't."

"I think we might," he countered, stubbornly refusing to hand over the cuff link.

Fine. Let him keep it. She had better things to do, like help lovebirds snap selfies while trying on rings. Anything to extricate herself from the current situation.

She flew to her feet. "Everything seems in order here. I'll just be going…"

"Diana, wait." Artem was using his CEO voice. Marvelous.

She obediently stayed put, lest he rethink his promise and banish her to an eternity of working in Engagements.

Franco took his time unfolding himself to a standing position, as if everyone was happy to wait for him, the Manhattan sunset included.

"Mr. Andrade, I'm Artem Drake, CEO of Drake Diamonds." Artem gestured toward Diana. "And this is my sister, Diana Drake."

"It's a pleasure to meet you," she said tightly and crossed her arms.

Artem shot her a reproachful glare. With no small amount of reluctance, she pasted on a smile and offered her hand for a shake.

Franco's gaze dropped to her outstretched fingertips. He waited a beat until her cheeks flared with heat, then dropped the cuff link into her palm without touching her.

"El gusto es mio," he said with just a hint of an Argentine accent.

The pleasure is mine.

A rebellious shiver ran down Diana's spine.

That shiver didn't mean anything. Of course it didn't. He was a beautiful man, that was all. It was only natural for her body to respond to that kind of physical perfection, even though her head knew better than to pay any attention to his broad shoulders and dark, glittering eyes.

She swallowed. Overwhelming character flaws aside, Franco Andrade had always been devastatingly handsome... emphasis on *devastating*.

It was hardly fair. But life wasn't always fair, was it? No, it most definitely wasn't. Lately, it had been downright cruel.

Diana's throat grew thick. She had difficulty swallowing all of a sudden. Then, somewhere amid the sudden fog in her head, she became aware of Artem clearing his throat.

"Shall we get started? I believe we're chasing the light." He introduced Franco to the photographer, who practically swooned on the spot when he turned his gaze on her.

Diana suppressed a gag and did her best to blend into the Drake-blue walls.

Apparently, any and all attempts at disappearing proved futile. As she tried to make an escape, Artem motioned her back. "Diana, join us please."

She forced her lips into something resembling a smile and strode toward the window where the photographer was getting Franco into position with a wholly unnecessary amount of hands-on attention. The woman with the camera had clearly forgiven him for his tardiness. It figured.

Diana turned her back on the nauseating scene and raised an eyebrow at Artem, who was tapping away on his iPhone. "You needed me?"

He looked up from his cell. "Yes. Can you get Mr. Andrade fitted with some cuff links?"

She stared blankly at him. "Um, me?"

"Yes, you." He shrugged. "What's with the attitude? I thought you'd be pleased. I'm talking to the same person who just stormed into my office demanding a different job than working in Engagements, right?"

She swallowed. "Yes. Yes, of course."

She longed to return to her dreadful post, but if she did, Artem would never take her seriously. Not after everything she'd said earlier.

"Cuff links." She nodded. "I'm on it."

She could do this. She absolutely could. She was Diana

Drake, for crying out loud. She had a reputation all over the world for being fearless.

At least, that's what people used to say about her. Not so much anymore.

Just do it and get it over with. You'll never see him again after today. Those days are over.

She squared her shoulders, grabbed a pair of cuff links and marched toward the corner of the room that had been roped off for the photo shoot, all the while fantasizing about the day when she'd be the one in charge of this place. Or at least not at the very bottom of the food chain.

Franco leaned languidly against the window while the photographer tousled his dark hair, ostensibly for styling purposes.

"Excuse me." Diana held up the cuff links—18-carat white-gold knots covered in black pavé diamonds worth more than half the engagement rings in the room. "I've got the jewels."

"Excellent," the photographer chirped. "I'll grab the camera and we'll be good to go."

She ran her hand through Franco's hair one final time before sauntering away.

If Franco noticed the sudden, exaggerated swing in her hips, he didn't let it show. He fixed his gaze pointedly at Diana. "You've come to dress me?"

"No." Her face went instantly hot. Again. "I mean, yes. Sort of."

The corner of his mouth tugged into a provocative grin and he offered her his wrists.

She reached for one of his shirt cuffs, and her mortification reached new heights when she realized her hands were shaking.

Will this day ever end?

"Be still, *mi cielo*," he whispered, barely loud enough for her to hear.

Mi cielo.

She knew the meaning of those words because he'd whispered them to her before. Back then, she'd clung to them as if they'd meant something.

Mi cielo. My heaven.

They hadn't, though. They'd meant nothing to him. Neither had she.

"I'm not yours, Mr. Andrade. Never have been, never will be." She glared at him, jammed the second cuff link into his shirt with a little too much force and dropped his wrist. "We're finished here."

Why did she have the sinking feeling that she might be lying?

Chapter Two

Diana Drake didn't remember him. Or possibly she did, and she despised him. Franco wasn't altogether sure which prospect was more tolerable.

The idea of being so easily forgotten didn't sit well. Then again, being memorable hadn't exactly done him any favors lately, had it?

No, he thought wryly. *Not so much*. But it had been a hell of a lot of fun. At least, while it had lasted.

Fun wasn't part of his vocabulary anymore. Those days had ended. He was starting over with a clean slate, a new chapter and whatever other metaphors applied.

Not that he'd had much of a choice in the matter.

He'd been fired. Let go. Dumped from the Kingsmen Polo Team. Jack Ellis, the owner of the Kingsmen, had finally made good on all the ultimatums he'd issued over the years. It probably shouldn't have come as a surprise.

Franco knew he'd pushed the limits of Ellis's tolerance. More than once. More than a few times, to be honest.

But he'd never let his extracurricular activities affect his performance on the field. Franco had been the Kingsmen's record holder for most goals scored for four years running. His season total was always double the number of the next closest player on the list.

Which made his dismissal all the more frustrating, particularly considering he hadn't actually broken any rules. This time, Franco had been innocent. For probably the first time in his adult life, he'd done nothing untoward.

The situation dripped with so much irony that Franco was practically swimming in it. He would have found the entire turn of events amusing if it hadn't been so utterly frustrating.

"Mr. Andrade, could you lift your right forearm a few inches?" the photographer asked. "Like this."

She demonstrated for him, and Franco dragged his gaze away from Diana Drake with more reluctance than he cared to consider. He hadn't been watching her intentionally. His attention just kept straying in her direction. Again and again, for some strange reason.

She wasn't the most beautiful woman he'd ever seen. Then again, beautiful women were a dime a dozen in his world. There was something far more intriguing about Diana Drake than her appearance.

Although it didn't hurt to look at her. On the contrary, Franco rather enjoyed the experience.

She stood at one of the jewelry counters arranging and rearranging her tiny row of cuff links. He wondered if she realized her posture gave him a rather spectacular view of her backside. Judging by the way she seemed intent on ignoring him, he doubted it. She wasn't posing for his benefit, like, say, the photographer seemed to be doing. Franco could tell when a woman was trying to get his attention, and this one wasn't.

He couldn't quite put his finger on what it was about her that captivated him until she stole a glance at him from across the room.

The memory hit him like a blow to the chest.

Those eyes…

Until he'd met Diana, Franco had never seen eyes that color before—deep violet. They glittered like amethysts. Framed by thick ebony lashes, they were in such startling contrast with her alabaster complexion that he couldn't quite bring himself to look away. Even now.

And that was a problem. A big one.

"Mr. Andrade," the photographer repeated. "Your wrist."

He adjusted his posture and shot her an apologetic wink. The photographer's cheeks went pink, and he knew he'd been forgiven. Franco glanced at Diana again, just in time to see her violet eyes rolling in disgust.

A problem. Most definitely.

He had no business noticing *any* woman right now, particularly one who bore the last name Drake. He was on the path to redemption, and the Drakes were instrumental figures on that path. As such, Diana Drake was strictly off-limits.

So it was a good thing she clearly didn't want to give him the time of day. What a relief.

Right.

Franco averted his gaze from Diana Drake's glittering violet eyes and stared into the camera.

"Perfect," the photographer cooed. "Just perfect."

Beside her, Artem Drake nodded. "Yes, this is excellent. But maybe we should mix it up a little before we lose the light."

The photographer lowered her camera and glanced around the showroom, filled with engagement rings. You couldn't swing a polo mallet in the place without hitting a dozen diamond solitaires. "What were you thinking? Something romantic, maybe?"

"We've done romantic." Artem shrugged. "Lots of times. I was hoping for something a little more eye-catching."

The photographer frowned. "Let me think for a minute."

A generous amount of furtive murmuring followed, and Franco sighed. He'd known modeling wouldn't be as exciting as playing polo. He wasn't an idiot. But he'd been on the job for less than an hour and he was already bored out of his mind.

He sighed. Again.

His eyes drifted shut, and he imagined he was someplace else. Someplace that smelled of hay and horses and churned-up earth. Someplace where the ground shook with the thunder of hooves. Someplace where he never felt restless or boxed in.

The pounding that had begun in his temples subsided ever so slightly. When he opened his eyes, Diana Drake was standing mere inches away.

Franco smiled. "We meet again."

Diana's only response was a visible tensing of her shoulders as the photographer gave her a push and shoved her even closer toward him.

"Okay, now turn around. Quickly before the sun sets," the photographer barked. She turned her attention toward Franco. "Now put your arms around her. Pull her close, right up against your body. Yes, like that. Perfect!"

Diana obediently situated herself flush against him, with her lush bottom fully pressed against his groin. At last things were getting interesting.

Maybe he didn't hate modeling so much, after all.

Franco cleared his throat. "Well, this is awkward," he whispered, sending a ripple through Diana's thick dark hair.

He tried his best not to think about how soft that hair felt against his cheek or how much her heady floral scent reminded him of buttery-yellow orchids growing wild on the vine in Argentina.

"Awkward?" Diana shot him a glare over her shoulder. "From what I hear, you're used to this kind of thing."

He tightened his grip on her tiny waist. "And here I thought you didn't remember me."

"You're impossible," Diana said under her breath, wiggling uncomfortably in his arms.

"That's not what you said the last time we were in this position."

"Oh, my God, you did *not* just say that." This was the Diana Drake he remembered. Fiery. Bold.

"Nice." Artem strode toward them, nodding. "I like it. Against the sunset, you two look gorgeous. Edgy. Intimate."

Diana shook her head. "Artem, you're not serious."

"Actually, I am. Here." He lifted his hand. A sparkling diamond and sapphire necklace dangled from it with a center stone nearly as large as a polo ball. "Put this around your neck, Diana."

Diana crossed her arms. "Really, I'm not sure I should be part of this."

"It's just one picture out of hundreds. We probably won't even use it. The campaign is for cuff links, remember? Humor me, sis. Put it on." He arched a brow. "Besides, I thought you were interested in exploring other career opportunities around here."

She snatched the jewels out of his hands. "Fine."

Career opportunities?

"You're not working here, are you?" Franco murmured, barely loud enough for her to hear.

Granted, her last name was Drake. But why on earth would she give up a grand prix riding career to peddle diamonds?

"As a matter of fact, I am," she said primly.

"Why? If memory serves, you belong on a medal stand. Not here."

"Why do you care?" she asked through clenched teeth as the photographer snapped away.

Good question. "I don't."

"Fine."

But it wasn't fine. He *did* care, damn it. He shouldn't, but he did.

He would have given his left arm to be on horseback right now, and Diana Drake was working as a salesgirl when she could have been riding her way to the Olympics. What was she thinking? "It just seems like a phenomenal waste of talent. Be honest. You miss it, don't you?"

Her fingertips trembled and she nearly dropped the necklace down her blouse.

Franco covered her hands with his. "Here, let me help."

"I can do it," she snapped.

Franco sighed. "Look, the faster we get this picture taken, the faster all this will be over."

He bowed his head to get a closer look at the catch on the necklace, and his lips brushed perilously close to the elegant curve of her neck. She glanced at him over her shoulder, and for a sliver of a moment, her gaze dropped to his mouth. She let out a tremulous breath, and Franco could have sworn he heard a kittenish noise escape her lips.

Her reaction aroused him more than it should have, which he blamed on his newfound celibacy.

This lifestyle was going to prove more challenging than he'd anticipated.

But that was okay. Franco had never been the kind of man who backed down from a challenge. On the contrary, he relished it. He'd always played his best polo when facing his toughest opponents. Adversity brought out the best in Franco. He'd learned that lesson the hard way.

A long time ago.

Another time, another place.

"You two are breathtaking," the photographer said. "Diana, open the collar of your blouse just a bit so we can get a better view of the sapphire."

She obeyed, and Franco found himself momentarily spellbound by the graceful contours of her collarbones. Her skin was lovely. Luminous and pale beside the brilliant blue of the sapphire around her neck.

"Okay, I think we've got it." The photographer lowered her camera.

"We're finished?" Diana asked.

"Yes, all done."

"Excellent." She started walking away without so much as a backward glance.

"Aren't you forgetting something, *mi cielo*?" he said.

She spun back around, face flushed. He'd seen her wear that same heated expression during competition. "What?"

He held up his wrists. "Your cuff links."

"Oh. Um. Yes, thank you." She unfastened them and

gathered them in her closed fist. "Goodbye, Mr. Andrade."

She squared her shoulders and slipped past him. All business.

But Franco wasn't fooled. He'd seen the tremble in her fingertips as she'd loosened the cuffs of his shirt. She'd been shaking like a leaf, which struck him as profoundly odd.

Diana may have pretended to forget him, but he remembered her all too well. There wasn't a timid bone in her body, which had made her beyond memorable. She was confidence personified. It was one of the qualities that made her such an excellent rider.

If Diana Drake was anything, it was fearless. In the best possible way. She possessed the kind of tenacity that couldn't be taught. It was natural. Inborn. Like a person's height. Or the tone of her voice.

Or eyes the color of violets.

But people changed, didn't they? It happened all the time.

It had to. Franco was counting on it.

Chapter Three

Diana was running late for work.

Since the day of the mortifying photo shoot, she'd begun to dread the tenth-floor showroom with more fervor than ever before. Every time she looked up from one of the jewelry cases, she half expected to see Franco Andrade strolling toward her with a knowing look in his eyes and a smug grin on his handsome face. It was a ridiculous thing to worry about, of course. He had no reason to return to the store. The photo shoot was over. Finished.

Thank goodness.

Besides, if history had proven anything, it was that Franco wasn't fond of follow-through.

Still, she couldn't quite seem to shake the memory of how it had felt when he fastened that sapphire pendant around her neck…the graze of his fingertips on her collarbone, the tantalizing warmth of his breath on her skin.

It had been a long time since Diana had been touched in such an intimate way. A very long time. She knew getting her photo taken with Franco hadn't been real. They'd been posing, that's all. Pretending. She wasn't delusional, for heaven's sake.

But her body clearly hadn't been on the same page as her head. Physically, she'd been ready to believe the beautiful lie. She'd bought it, hook, line and sinker.

Just as she'd done the night she'd slept with him.

It was humiliating to think about the way she'd reacted to seeing him again after so long. She'd practically melted into a puddle at the man's feet. And not just any man. Franco Andrade was the king of the one night stand.

Even worse, she was fairly sure he'd known. He'd noticed the hitch in her breath, the flutter of her heart, the way she'd burned. He'd noticed, and he'd enjoyed it. Every mortifying second.

Don't think about it. It's over and done. Besides, it wasn't even a thing. It was nothing.

Except the fact that she kept thinking about it made it feel like something. A very big, very annoying something.

Enough. She had more important things to worry about than embarrassing herself in front of that polo-playing lothario. It hadn't been the first time, after all. She'd made an idiot out of herself in his presence before and lived to tell about it. At least this time she'd managed to keep her clothes on.

She tightened her grip on the silver overhead bar as the subway car came to a halt. The morning train was as crowded as ever, and when the doors slid open she wiggled her way toward the exit through a crush of commuters.

She didn't realize she'd gotten off at the wrong stop until it was too late.

Perfect. Just perfect. She was already running late, and now she'd been so preoccupied by Franco Andrade that she'd somehow gotten off the subway at the most crowded spot in New York. Times Square.

She slipped her messenger bag over her shoulder and climbed the stairs to street level. The trains had been running slow all morning, and she'd never be on time now. She might as well walk the rest of the way. A walk would do her good. Maybe the spring air would help clear her head and banish all thoughts of Franco once and for all.

It was worth a shot, anyway.

Diana took a deep inhale and allowed herself to remember how much she'd always loved to ride during this time of year. No more biting wind in her face. No more frost on the ground. In springtime, the sun glistened off her horse's ebony coat until it sparkled like black diamonds.

Diana's chest grew tight. She swallowed around the lump in her throat and fought the memories, pushed them back to the farthest corner of her mind where they belonged. *Don't cry. Don't do it.* If she did, she might not be able to stop.

After everything that had happened, she didn't want to be the pitiful-looking woman weeping openly on the sidewalk.

She focused, instead, on the people around her. Whenever the memory of the accident became too much, she tried her best to focus outward rather than on what was going on inside. Once, at Drake Diamonds, she'd stared at a vintage-inspired engagement ring for ten full minutes until the panic had subsided. She'd counted every tiny diamond in its art deco pavé setting, traced each slender line of platinum surrounding the central stone.

When she'd been in the hospital, her doctor had told her she might not remember everything that had led up to her fall. Most of the time, people with head injuries suffered memory loss around the time of impact. They didn't remember what had happened right before they'd been hurt.

They were the lucky ones.

Diana remembered everything. She would have given anything to forget.

Breathe in, breathe out. Look around you.

The streets were crowded with pedestrians, and as Diana wove her way through the crush of people, she thought she caught a few of them looking at her. They nodded and smiled in apparent recognition.

What was going on?

She was accustomed to being recognized at horse shows. On the riding circuit she'd been a force to be reckoned with. But this wasn't the Hamptons or Connecticut. This was Manhattan. She should blend in here. That was one of the things she liked best about the city—a person could just disappear right in the middle of a crowd. She didn't have to perform here. She could be anyone.

At least that's how she'd felt until Franco Andrade had walked into Drake Diamonds. The moment she'd set eyes on him, the dividing line between her old life and her new one had begun to blur.

She didn't like it. Not one bit. Before he'd shown up, she'd been doing a pretty good job of keeping things compartmentalized. She'd started a new job. She'd spent her evening hours in Dalton's apartment watching television until she fell asleep. She'd managed to live every day without giving much thought to what she was missing.

But the moment Franco had touched her she'd known the truth. She wasn't okay. The accident had affected her more than she could admit, even to herself.

There'd been an awareness in the graze of his fingertips, a strange intimacy in the way he'd looked at her. As if she were keeping a secret that only he was privy to. She'd felt exposed. Vulnerable. Seen.

She'd always felt that way around Franco, which is why she'd been stupid enough to end up in his bed. The way she felt when he looked at her had been intoxicating back then. Impossible to ignore.

But she didn't want to be seen now. Not anymore. She just wanted to be invisible for a while.

Maybe she wouldn't have been so rattled if it had been someone else. But it had been *him*. And she was most definitely still shaken up.

She needed to get a grip. So she'd posed for a few pictures with a handsome man she used to know. That's all. Case closed. End of story. No big deal.

She squared her shoulders and marched down the street with renewed purpose. This was getting ridiculous. She would *not* let a few minutes with Franco ruin her new beginning. He meant nothing to her. She was only imagining things, anyway. He probably looked at every woman he met with that same knowing gleam in his eye. That's why they were always falling at his feet everywhere he went.

It was nauseating.

She wouldn't waste another second thinking about the man. She sighed and realized she was standing right in front of the Times Square Starbucks. Perfect. Coffee was just what she needed.

As soon as she took her place in line, a man across the room did a double take in her direction. His face broke into a wide smile. Diana glanced over her shoulder, convinced he was looking at someone behind her. His wife, maybe. Or a friend.

No one was there.

She turned back around. The man winked and raised his cardboard cup as if he were toasting her. Then he turned and walked out the door.

Diana frowned. People were weird. It was probably just some strange coincidence. Or the man was confused, that was all.

Except he didn't look confused. He looked perfectly friendly and sane.

"Can I help you?" The barista, a young man with wire-rimmed glasses and a close-cropped beard, jabbed at the cash register.

"Yes, please," Diana said. "I'd like a…"

The barista looked up, grinned and cut her off before she could place her order. "Oh, hey, you're that girl."

That girl?

Diana's gaze narrowed. She shook her head. "Um, I don't think I am."

What was she even arguing about? She didn't actually know. But she knew for certain that this barista shouldn't have any idea who she was.

Unless her accident had somehow ended up on YouTube or something.

Not that. Please not that.

Anything but that.

"Yeah, you are." The barista turned to the person in line behind her. "You know who she is too, right?"

Diana ventured a sideways glance at the woman, who didn't look the least bit familiar. Diana was sure she'd never seen her before.

"Of course." The woman looked Diana up and down. "You're her. Most definitely."

For a split second, relief washed over her. She wasn't losing it, after all. People on the sidewalk really had been staring at her. The triumphant feeling was short-lived when she realized she still had no idea why.

"Will one of you please tell me what's going on? What girl?"

The woman and the barista exchanged a glance.

"The girl from the billboard," the woman said.

Diana blinked.

The girl from the billboard.

This couldn't be about the photos she'd taken with Franco. It just couldn't. Artem was her brother. He wouldn't slap a picture of her on a Drake Diamonds billboard without her permission. Of course he wouldn't.

Would he?

Diana looked back and forth between the woman and the barista. "What billboard?"

She hated how shaky and weak her voice sounded, so she repeated herself. This time she practically screamed. *"What billboard?"*

The woman flinched, and Diana immediately felt horrible. Her new life apparently included having her face on billboards and yelling at random strangers in coffee shops. It wasn't exactly the fresh start she'd imagined for herself.

"It's right outside. Take two steps out the front door and look up. You can't miss it." The barista lifted a brow. "Are you going to order something or what? You're holding up the line."

"No, thank you." She couldn't stomach a latte right now. Simply putting one foot in front of the other seemed like a monumental task.

She scooted out of line and made her way to the door. She paused for a moment before opening it, hoping for one final, naive second that this was all some big mistake. Maybe Artem hadn't used the photo of her and Franco for the new campaign. Maybe the billboard they'd seen wasn't even a Drake Diamonds advertisement. Maybe it was an ad for some other company with a model who just happened to look like Diana.

That was possible, wasn't it?

But deep down she knew it wasn't, and she had no one to blame but herself.

She'd stormed into Artem's office and demanded that he find a role for her in the company that didn't involve Engagements. She'd practically gotten down on her knees and begged. He'd given her exactly what she wanted. She just hadn't realized that being on a billboard alongside Franco Andrade in the middle of Times Square was part of the equation.

She took a deep breath.

It was just a photograph. She and Franco weren't a couple or anything. They were simply on a billboard together. A million people would probably walk right past it and never notice. By tomorrow it would be old news. She was getting all worked up over nothing.

How bad could it be?

She walked outside, looked up and got her answer.

It was bad. Really, really bad.

Emblazoned across the top of the Times Tower was a photo of herself being embraced from behind by Franco. The sapphire necklace dangled from his fingertips, but rather than looking like he was helping her put it on, the photo gave the distinct impression he was removing it.

Franco's missing tie and the unbuttoned collar of his

tuxedo shirt didn't help matters. Neither did her flushed cheeks and slightly parted lips.

This wasn't an advertisement for cuff links. It looked more like an ad for sex. If she hadn't known better, Diana would have thought the couple in the photograph was just a heartbeat away from falling into bed together.

And she and Franco Andrade were that couple.

What have I done?

Franco was trying his level best not pummel Artem Drake.

But it was hard. Really hard.

"I didn't sign up for this." He wadded the flimsy newsprint of *Page Six* in his hands and threw it at Artem, who was seated across from Franco in the confines of his Drake-blue office. "Selling cuff links, yes. Selling sex, no."

Artem had the decency to flinch at the mention of sex, but Franco was guessing that was mostly out of a brotherly sense of propriety. After all, his sister was the one who looked as though Franco was seducing her on the cover of every tabloid in the western hemisphere.

From what Franco had heard, there was even a billboard smack in the middle of Times Square. His phone had been blowing up with texts and calls all morning. Regrettably, not a single one of those texts or calls had included an offer to return to the Kingsmen.

"Mr. Andrade, please calm down." Artem waved a hand at the generous stack of newspapers fanned across the surface of his desk. "The new campaign was unveiled just hours ago, and it's already a huge success. I've made you famous. You're a household name. People who've never seen a polo match in their lives know who you are. This is what you wanted, is it not?"

Yes…

And no.

He'd wanted to get Jack Ellis's attention. To force his hand. Just not like this.

But he couldn't explain the details of his reinvention to Artem Drake. His new "employer" didn't even know he'd been cut from the team. To Franco's knowledge, no one did. And if he had anything to say about it, no one would. Because he'd be back in his jersey before the first game of the season in Bridgehampton.

That was the plan, anyway.

He stared at the pile of tabloids on Artem's desk. Weeks of clean living and celibacy had just been flushed straight down the drain. More importantly, so had his one shot at getting his life back.

He glared at Artem. "Surely you can't be happy about the fact that everyone in the city thinks I'm sleeping with your sister."

A subtle tension in the set of Artem's jaw was the only crack in his composure. "She's a grown woman, not a child."

"So I've noticed." It was impossible not to.

A lot could happen in three years. She'd been young when she'd shared Franco's bed. Naive. Blissfully so. If he'd realized how innocent she was, he never would have touched her.

But all that was water under the bridge.

Just like Franco's career.

"Besides, this—" Artem gestured toward the pile of newspapers "—isn't real. It's an illusion. One that's advantageous to both of us."

This guy was unbelievable. And he was clearly unaware that Franco and Diana shared a past. Which was probably for the best, given the circumstances.

Franco couldn't help but be intrigued by what he was saying, though. *Advantageous to both of us…*

"Do explain."

Artem shrugged. *Yep, clueless.* "I'm no stranger to the tabloids. Believe me, I understand where you're coming from. But there's a way to use this kind of exposure and make the most out of it. We've managed to get the attention of the world. Our next step is keeping it."

He already didn't like the sound of this. "What exactly are you proposing?"

"A press tour. Take the cuff links out for a spin. You make the rounds of the local philanthropy scene—black-tie parties, charity events, that sort of thing—and smile for the cameras." His gaze flitted to the photo of Franco and Diana. "Alongside my sister, of course."

"Let me get this straight. You want to pay me to publically date Diana." No way in hell. He was an athlete, not a gigolo.

"Absolutely not. I want to pay you to make appearances while wearing Drake gemstones. If people happen to assume you and Diana are a couple, so be it."

Franco narrowed his gaze. "You know they will."

Artem shrugged. "Let them. Look, I didn't plan any of this. But we'd all be fools not to take advantage of the buzz. From what I hear, appearing to be in a monogamous relationship could only help your reputation."

Ah, so the cat was out of the bag, after all.

Franco cursed under his breath. "How long do you expect me to keep up this farce?"

He wasn't sure why he was asking. It was a completely ludicrous proposition.

Although he supposed there were worse fates than spending time with Diana Drake.

Don't go there. Not again.

"Twenty-one days," Artem said.

Franco knew the date by heart already. "The day before the American polo season starts in Bridgehampton. The Kingsmen go on tour right after the season starts."

"Precisely. And you'll be going with them. Assuming you're back on the team by then, obviously." Artem shrugged. "That's what you want, isn't it?"

Franco wondered how Artem had heard about his predicament. He hadn't thought the news of his termination had spread beyond the polo community. Somehow the fact that it had made it seem more real. Permanent.

And that was unacceptable.

"It's absolutely what I want," he said.

"Good. Let us help you fix your reputation." Artem shrugged as if doing so was just that simple.

Maybe it is. "I don't understand. What would you be getting out of this proposed arrangement? Are you really this desperate to move your cuff links?"

"Hardly. This is about more than cuff links." Artem rummaged around the stack of gossip rags on his desk until he found a neatly folded copy of the *New York Times.* "Much more."

He slid the paper across the smooth surface of the desk. It didn't take long for Franco to spot the headline of interest: Jewelry House to be Chosen for World's Largest Uncut Diamond.

Franco looked up and met Artem's gaze. "Let me guess. Drake Diamonds wants to cut this diamond."

"Of course we do. The stone is over one thousand carats. It's the size of a baseball. Every jewelry house in Manhattan wants to get its hands on it. Once it's been cut and placed in a setting, the diamond will be unveiled at a gala at the Metropolitan Museum of Art. Followed by a featured exhibition open to the public, naturally."

Franco's eyes narrowed. "Would the date for this gala possibly be twenty-one days from now?"

"Bingo." Artem leaned forward in his chair. "It's the perfect arrangement. You and Diana will keep Drake Diamonds on the front page of every newspaper in New York. The owners of the diamond will see the Drake name everywhere they turn, and they'll have no choice but to pick us as their partners."

"I see." It actually made sense. In a twisted sort of way.

Artem continued, "By the time you and Diana attend the Met's diamond gala together, you'll have been in a high-profile relationship for nearly a month. Monogamous. Respectable. You're certain to get back in the good graces of your team."

Maybe. Then again, maybe not.

"Plus you'll be great for the team's ticket sales. The more famous you are, the more people will line up to see you play. The Kingsmen will be bound to forgive and forget whatever transgression got you fired." Artem lifted a brow. "What exactly did you do, anyway? You're the best player on the circuit, so it couldn't have been related to your performance on the field."

Franco shrugged. "I didn't do anything, actually."

He'd been cut through no fault of his own. Even worse, he'd been unable to defend himself. Telling the lie had been his choice, though. His call. He'd done what he'd needed to do.

It had been a matter of honor. Even if he'd been able to go back in time and erase the past thirty days, he'd still do it all over again.

Make the same choice. Say the same things.

Artem regarded him through narrowed eyes. "Fine.

You don't need to tell me. From now on, you're a reformed man, anyway. Nothing else matters."

"Got it." Franco nodded.

He wasn't seriously considering this arrangement. It was borderline demeaning, wasn't it? To both himself and Diana.

Diana Drake.

He could practically hear her breathy, judgmental voice in his ear. *From what I hear, you're used to this kind of thing.*

She'd never go along with this charade. She had too much pride. Then again, what did he know about Diana Drake these days?

He cleared his throat. "What happens afterward?"

"Afterward?"

Franco nodded. "Yes, after the gala."

Artem smiled. "I'm assuming you'll ride off into the sunset with your team and score a massive amount of goals. You'll continue to behave professionally and eventually you and Diana will announce a discreet breakup."

They'd never get away with it. Diana hadn't even set eyes on Franco or deigned to speak a word to him in the past three years until just a few days ago. No one would seriously believe they were a couple.

He stared down at the heap of newspapers on Artem's desk.

People already believed it.

"You'll be compensated for each appearance at the rate we agreed upon under the terms of your modeling contract. You can start tonight."

"Tonight?"

Artem gave a firm nod. "The Manhattan Pet Rescue animal shelter is holding its annual Fur Ball at the Waldorf Astoria. You and Diana can dress up and cuddle with a few adorable puppies and kittens. Every photographer in town will be there."

The Fur Ball. It certainly sounded wholesome. Nauseatingly, mind-numbingly adorable.

"I'm assuming we have a deal." Artem stood.

Franco rose from his seat, but ignored Artem's outstretched hand. They couldn't shake on things. Not yet. "You're forgetting something."

"What's that?"

Not what. Who. "Diana. She'll never agree to this."

Artem's gaze grew sharp. Narrow. "What makes you say so?"

Franco had a sudden memory of her exquisite violet eyes, shiny with unshed tears as she slapped him hard across the face. "Trust me. She won't."

"Just be ready for the driver to pick you up at eight. I'll handle Diana." Artem offered his hand again.

This time, Franco took it.

But even as they shook on the deal, he knew it would never happen. Diana wasn't the sort of person who could be handled. By anyone. Artem Drake had no idea what he was up against. Franco almost felt sorry for him. Almost, but not quite.

Some things could only be learned the hard way.

Like a slap in the face.

Chapter Four

Diana called Artem repeatedly on her walk to Drake Diamonds, but his secretary refused to put her through. She kept insisting that he was in an important business meeting and had left instructions not to be disturbed, which only made Diana angrier. If such a thing was even possible.

A billboard. In Times Square.

She wanted to die.

Calm down. Just breathe. People will forget all about it in a day or two. In the grand scheme of life, it's not that big a deal.

But there was no deluding herself. It was, quite literally, a big deal. A huge one. A whopping 25,000-square-foot Technicolor enormous deal.

Artem would have to take it down. That's all there was to it. She hadn't signed any kind of modeling release. Drake might be her last name, but that didn't mean the family business owned the rights to her likeness.

Or did it? She wasn't even sure. Drake Diamonds had been her sponsor on the equestrian circuit. Maybe the business did, in fact, own her.

God, why hadn't she gone to college? She was in no way prepared for this.

She pushed her way through the revolving door of Drake Diamonds with a tad too much force. Urgent meeting or not, Artem was going to talk to her. She'd break down the door of his Drake-blue office if that's what it took.

"Whoa, there." The door spun too quickly and hurled her toward some poor, unsuspecting shopper in the lobby who caught her by the shoulders before she crashed into him. "Slow down, Wildfire."

"Sorry. I just…" She straightened, blinked and found herself face-to-face with the poster boy himself. Franco. "Oh, it's you."

What was he doing here? *Again?* And why were his hands on her shoulders? And why was he calling her that ridiculous name?

Wildfire.

She'd loved that song when she was a little girl. So, so much.

Well, she didn't love it anymore. In fact, Franco had just turned her off it for life.

"Good morning to you too, Diana." He winked. He was probably the only man on planet Earth who could make such a cheesy gesture seem charming.

Ugh.

She wiggled out of his grasp. "Why are you here? Wait, don't tell me. You're snapping selfies for the Drake Diamonds Instagram."

He was wearing a suit. Not a tuxedo this time, but a finely tailored suit, nonetheless. It was weird seeing him dressed this way. Shouldn't he be wearing riding clothes? He adjusted his shirt cuffs. "It bothers you that I'm the new face of Drake Diamonds?"

"No, it doesn't actually. I couldn't care less what you do. It bothers me that *I'm* the new face of Drake Diamonds." A few shoppers with little blue bags dangling from their wrists turned and stared.

Franco angled his head closer to hers. "You might want to keep your voice down."

"I don't care who hears me." She was being ridiculous. But she couldn't quite help it, and she certainly wasn't going to let Franco tell her how to behave.

"Your brother will care," he said.

"What are you talking about?" Then she put two and two together. Finally. "Wait a minute…were you just upstairs with Artem?"

He nodded. Diana must have been imagining things, because he almost looked apologetic.

"So you're the reason his secretary wouldn't put my calls through?" Unbelievable.

"I suppose so, yes." Again, something about his expression was almost contrite.

She glared at him. He could be as nice as he wanted, but as far as Diana was concerned, it was too little, too late. "What was this urgent tête-à-tête about?"

Why was she asking him questions? She didn't care what he and Artem had to say to each other…

Except something about Franco's expression told her she should.

He leveled his gaze at her and arched a single seductive brow. Because, yes, even the man's eyebrows were sexy. "I think you should talk to Artem."

She swallowed. Something was going on here. Something big. And she had the distinct feeling she wasn't going to like it. "Fine. But just so we're clear, I'm talking to him because I want to. And because he's my brother and sort of my boss. Not because you're telling me I should."

"Duly noted." He seemed to be struggling not to smile.

She lifted her chin in defiance. "Goodbye, Franco."

But for some reason, her feet didn't move. She just kept standing there, gazing up at his despicably handsome face.

"See you tonight, Wildfire." He shot her a knowing half grin before turning for the door.

She stood frozen, gaping after him.

Tonight?

She definitely needed to talk to Artem. Immediately.

She skipped the elevator and took the stairs two at a time until she reached the tenth floor, where she found him sitting at his desk as if it was any ordinary day. A day when Franco Andrade wasn't wandering the streets of Manhattan wearing Tom Ford and planning on seeing her tonight.

"Hello, sis." Artem looked up and frowned as he took in her appearance. "Why do you look like you just ran a marathon?"

"Because I just walked a few miles, then sprinted up the stairs." She was breathless. Her legs burned, which was just wrong. She shouldn't be winded from a little exercise. She was an elite athlete.

Used to be an elite athlete.

He gestured toward the wingback chair opposite him. "Take a load off. I need to talk to you, anyway."

"So I've heard." She didn't want to sit down. She wanted to stand and scream at him, but that wasn't going to get her anywhere. Besides, she felt drained all of a sudden. Being around Franco, even for a few minutes, was exhausting. "Speaking of which, what was Franco Andrade doing here just now?"

"About that…" He calmly folded his hands in front of him, drawing Diana's attention first to the smooth surface of his desk and then to the oddly huge stack of newspapers on top of it.

She blinked and cut him off midsentence. "Is that my picture on the front page of the *New York Daily News*?"

She hadn't thought it possible for the day to get any worse, but it just had. So much worse.

And the hits kept on coming. As she sifted through the stack of tabloids—all of which claimed she was having a torrid affair with "the drop-dead gorgeous bad boy of polo"—Artem outlined his preposterous idea for a public relations campaign. Although it sounded more like an episode of *The Bachelor* than any kind of legitimate business plan.

"No, thank you." Diana flipped the copy of *Page Six* facedown so she wouldn't have to look at the photo of herself and Franco on the cover. If she never saw that picture again, it would be too soon.

Artem's brow furrowed. "No, thank you? What does that mean?"

"It means no. As in, I'll pass." What about her answer wasn't he understanding? She couldn't be more clear. "No. N.O."

"Perhaps you don't understand. We're talking about the largest uncut diamond in the world. Do you have any idea what this could mean for Drake Diamonds?" There was Artem's CEO voice again.

She wasn't about to let it intimidate her this time. "Yes. I realize it's very important, but we'll simply have to come up with another plan." *Preferably one that doesn't involve Franco Andrade in any way, shape or form.*

"Let's hear your suggestions, then." He leaned back in his chair and crossed his arms. "I'm all ears."

He wanted her to come up with a plan *now*?

Diana cleared her throat. "I'll have to give it some thought, obviously. But I'm sure I can come up with something."

"Go ahead. I'll wait."

"Artem, come on. We can take the owners of the diamond out to dinner or something. Wine and dine them."

"You realize every other jeweler in Manhattan is doing that exact same thing," he said.

Admittedly, that was probably true. "There's got to be a better way to catch their attention than letting everyone believe I'm having a scandalous affair with Franco."

Please let there be another way.

"Not scandalous. Just high profile. Romantic. Glamorous." Artem gave her a thoughtful look. "He told me you'd refuse, by the way. What, exactly, is the problem between you two?"

Diana swallowed. Maybe she should simply tell Artem what happened three years ago. Surely then he'd forget about parading her all over Park Avenue on Franco's arm just for the sake of a diamond. Even the biggest diamond in the known universe.

But she couldn't. She didn't even want to think about that humiliating episode, much less talk about it.

Especially to her brother, of all people.

"He's a complete and total man whore. You know that, right?" Wasn't that reason enough to turn down the opportunity to pretend date him for twenty-one days? "Aren't you at all concerned about my virtue?"

"The last time I checked, you were more than capable of taking care of yourself, Diana. In fact, you're one of the strongest women I know. I seriously doubt I need to worry about your virtue." He shrugged. "But I could have a word with Franco...do the whole brother thing and threaten him with bodily harm if he lays a finger on you. Would that make you feel better?"

"God, no." She honestly couldn't fathom anything more mortifying.

"It's your call." Artem shrugged. "He's rehabilitating his image, anyway. Franco Andrade's man-whore days are behind him."

Diana laughed. Loud and hard. "He told you that? And you believed him?"

"When did you become such a cynic, sis?"

Three years ago. Right around the time I lost my virginity. "It seems dubious. That's all I'm saying. Why would he change after all this time, unless he's already had his way with every woman on the eastern seaboard?"

It was a distinct possibility.

"People change, Diana." His expression softened and he cast a meaningful glance at the bassinet in the corner of his office. A pink mobile hung over the cradle, decorated with tiny teddy bears wearing ballet shoes. "I did."

Diana smiled at the thought of her adorable baby niece.

He had a point. Less than a year ago, Artem had been the one on the cover of *Page Six*. He'd been photographed with a different woman every night. Now he was a candidate for father of the year.

Moreover, Diana had never seen a couple more in love than Artem and Ophelia. It was almost enough to restore her faith in marriage.

But not quite.

It would take more than her two brothers finding marital bliss to erase the memory of their father's numerous indiscretions.

It wasn't just the affairs. It was the way he'd made no

effort whatsoever to hide them from their mother. He'd expected her to accept it. To smile and look away. And she had.

Right up until the day she died.

She'd been just forty years old when Diana found her lifeless body on the living room floor. Still young, still beautiful. The doctors had been baffled. They'd been unable to find a reason for her sudden heart attack. But to Diana, the reason was obvious.

Her mother had died of a broken heart.

Was it any wonder she thought marriage was a joke? She was beyond screwed up when it came to relationships. How damaged must she have been to intentionally throw herself at a man who was famous for treating women as if they were disposable?

Diana squeezed her eyes shut.

Why did Franco have to come strutting back into her life *now*, while she was her most vulnerable? Before her accident, she could have handled him. She could have handled anything.

She opened her eyes. "Please, Artem. I just really, really don't want to do this."

He nodded. "I see. You'd rather spend all day, every day, slaving away in Engagements than attend a few parties with Franco. Understood. Sorry I brought it up."

He waved a hand toward the dreaded Engagements showroom down the hall. "Go ahead and get to work."

Diana didn't move a muscle. "Wait. Are you saying that if I play the part of Franco's fake girlfriend by night, I won't have to peddle engagement rings by day?"

She'd assumed her position in Engagements was still part of the plan. This changed things.

She swallowed. She still couldn't do it. She'd never

last a single evening in Franco's company, much less twenty-one of them.

Could she?

"Of course you wouldn't have to do both." Artem gestured toward the newspapers spread across his desk. "This would be a job, just like any other in the company."

She narrowed her gaze and steadfastly refused to look at the picture again. "What kind of job involves going to black-tie parties every night?"

"Vice president of public relations. I did it for years. The job is yours now, if you want it." He smiled. "You asked me to find something else for you to do, remember? Moving from the sales floor to a VP position is a meteoric rise."

When he put it that way, it didn't sound so bad. Vice president of public relations sounded pretty darn good, actually.

Finally. This was the kind of opportunity she'd been waiting for. She just never dreamed that Franco Andrade would be part of the package.

"I want a pay increase," she blurted.

What was she doing?

"Done." Artem's grin spread wide.

She wasn't seriously considering accepting the job though, was she? No. She couldn't. Wouldn't. No amount of money was worth her dignity.

But there was one thing that might make participating in the farce worthwhile…

"And if it works, I want to be promoted." She pasted on her sweetest smile. "Again."

Artem's brows rose. "You're going to have to be more specific. Besides, vice president is pretty high on the food chain around here."

"I'm aware. But this diamond gala is really important. You said so yourself."

Artem's smile faded. Just a bit. "That's right."

"If I do my part and Drake Diamonds is chosen as the jewelry house to cut the giant diamond and if everything goes off with a hitch at the Met's diamond gala, I think I deserve to take Dalton's place." She cleared her throat. "I want to be named co-CEO."

Artem didn't utter a word at first. He just sat and stared at her as if she'd sprouted another head.

Great. She'd pushed too far.

VP was a massive career leap. She should have jumped at the opportunity to put all the love-struck brides and grooms in the rearview mirror and left it at that.

"That's a bold request for someone with no business experience," he finally said.

"Correct me if I'm wrong, but wasn't vice president of public relations the only position you held at Drake Diamonds before our father died and appointed you his successor as CEO?" Did Artem really think she'd been so busy at horse shows that she had no clue what had gone on between these Drake-blue walls the past few years?

Still, what was she saying? He'd never buy into this.

He let out an appreciative laugh. "You're certainly shrewd enough for the job."

She grinned. "I'll take that as a compliment."

"As you should." He sighed, looked at her for a long, loaded moment and nodded. "Okay. It works for me."

She waited for some indication that he was joking, but it never came.

Her heart hammered hard in her chest. "Don't tease me, Artem. It's been kind of a rough day."

And it was about to get rougher.

If she and Artem had actually come to an agreement,

that meant she was going out with Franco Andrade tonight. By choice.

She needed to have her head examined.

"I'm not teasing. You made a valid point. I didn't know anything about being a CEO when I stepped into the position. I learned. You will, too." He held up a finger. A warning. "But only if you deliver. Drake Diamonds must be chosen to cut the stone and cosponsor the Met Diamond gala."

"No problem." She beamed at him.

For the first time since she'd fallen off her horse, she felt whole. Happy. She was building a new future for herself.

In less than a month, she'd be co-CEO. No more passing out petit fours. No more engagement rings. She'd never have to look at another copy of *Bride* magazine for as long as she lived!

Better yet, she wouldn't have to answer any more questions about when she was going to start riding again. Every time she turned around, it seemed someone was asking her about her riding career. Had she gotten a new horse? Was she ready to start showing again?

Diana wasn't anywhere close to being ready. She wasn't sure she'd *ever* be ready.

Co-CEO was a big job. A huge responsibility—huge enough that it just might make people forget she'd once dreamed of going to the Olympics. If she was running the company alongside Artem, no one would expect her to compete anymore. It was the perfect solution.

She just had to get through the next twenty-one days first.

"Go home." Artem nodded toward his office door. "Rest up and get ready for tonight."

Tonight. A fancy party. The Waldorf Astoria. Franco.

She swallowed. "Everything will be fine."

Artem lifted a brow.

Had she really said that out loud?

"I know it will, because it's your job to make sure everything is fine," Artem said. "And for the record, there's not a doubt in my mind that your virtue is safe. You can hold your own, Diana. You just talked your way into a co-CEO job. From where I'm standing, if there's anyone who has reason to be afraid, it's Mr. Andrade."

He was right. She'd done that, hadn't she?

She could handle a few hours in Franco's company.

"I think you're right."

God, she hoped so.

Chapter Five

Franco leaned inside the Drake limo and did a double take when he saw Diana staring at him impassively from its dark interior.

"Buenas noches."

He'd expected the car to pick him up first and then take him to Diana's apartment so he could collect her. Like a proper date. But technically this wasn't a date, even though it already felt like one.

He couldn't remember the last time he'd dressed in a tuxedo and escorted a woman to a party. Despite his numerous exploits, Franco didn't often date. He arrived at events solo, and when the night was over he left with a woman on his arm. Sometimes several. Hours later, he typically went home alone. He rarely shared a bed with the same woman more than once, and he never spent the night. Ever.

In fact, the last woman who'd woken up beside him had been Diana Drake.

"Good evening, yourself," she said, without bothering to give him more than a cursory glance.

That would have to change once they arrived at the gala. Lovers looked at each other. They touched each other. Hell, if Diana was his lover, Franco wouldn't be able to keep his hands off her.

This isn't real.

He slid onto the smooth leather seat beside her.

It wasn't real, but it felt real. It even looked real.

Diana was dressed in a strapless chiffon gown, midnight blue, with a dangerously low, plunging neckline. A glittering stone rested between her breasts. A sapphire. *The* sapphire necklace from the photo shoot.

"Please stop staring." She turned and met his gaze. At last.

Franco's body hardened the instant his eyes fixed on hers. As exquisite as the sapphire around her neck was, it didn't hold a candle to the luminescent violet depths of those eyes. "You're lovely."

She stared at him coldly. "Save it for the cameras, would you? There's no one here. You can drop the act."

"It's not an act. You look beautiful." He swallowed. Hard. "That's quite a dress."

He was used to seeing her in riding clothes, not like this. He couldn't seem to look away.

What are you, a teenager? Grow up, Andrade.

"Seriously, stop." The car sped through a tunnel, plunging them into darkness. But the shadows couldn't hide the slight tremor in her voice. "Just stop it, would you? I know we're supposed to be madly in love with each other in public. But in private, can we keep things professional? Please?"

Something about the way she said *please* grabbed Franco by the throat and refused to let go.

Had he really been so awful to her all those years ago? Yes. He had.

Still, she'd been better off once he'd pushed her away, whether she'd realized it or not. She was an heiress. The real deal. And Franco wasn't the type of man she'd bring home.

Never had been, never would be.

"Professional. Got it," he said to the back of her head. It felt more like he was talking to himself than to Diana.

She'd turned away again, keeping her gaze fixed on the scenery outside the car window. The lights of the city rushed past, framing her silhouette in a dizzying halo of varying hues of gold.

They sat in stony silence down the lavish length of Park Avenue. The air in the limo felt so thick he was practically choking on it. Franco refrained from pointing out that refusing to either look at him or speak to him in something other than monosyllables was hardly professional.

Why the hell had she agreed to this arrangement, anyway? Neither one of them should be sitting in the back of a limo on the way to some boring gala. They both belonged on horseback. Franco knew why he wasn't training right now, but for the life of him, he couldn't figure out what Diana was doing working for her family business.

He was almost grateful when his phone chimed with an incoming text message, giving him something to focus on. Not looking at Diana was becoming more impossible by the second. She was stunning, even in her fury.

He slid his cell out of the inside pocket of his tuxedo jacket and looked at the screen.

A message from Luc. Again.

Ellis still isn't budging.

Franco's jaw clenched. That information wasn't exactly breaking news. If he'd held out any hope of the team owner changing his mind before the end of the day, he wouldn't be sitting beside the diamond ice princess right now.

Still, he didn't particularly enjoy dwelling on the dismal state of his career.

He moved to slip the phone back inside his pocket, but it chimed again.

This has gone on long enough.

And again.

I can't let you do this. I'm telling him the truth.

Damn it all to hell.
Franco tapped out a response…

Let it go. What's done is done. I have everything under control.

Beside him, Diana cleared her throat. "Lining up your date for the evening?"

Franco looked up and found her regarding him through narrowed eyes. She shot a meaningful glance at his phone.

So, she didn't like the thought of him texting other women? Interesting.

"You're my date for the evening, remember?" He wasn't texting another woman, obviously. But she didn't need to know that. He hardly owed her an explanation.

She rolled her eyes. "Don't even pretend you're going home alone after this."

He powered his phone down and glanced back up at Diana. "As a matter of fact, I am. Didn't Artem tell you? You and I are monogamous."

She arched a brow. "Did he explain what that meant, or did you have to look it up in the dictionary?"

"You're adorable when you're jealous. I like it." He was goading her, and he knew it. But at least they were speaking.

"If you think I'm jealous, you're even more full of yourself than I thought you were." In the darkened limousine, he could see two pink spots glowing on her cheeks. "Also, you're completely delusional."

He shrugged. "I disagree. Do you know why?"

"I can't begin to imagine what's going on inside your head. Nor would I want to." She exhaled a breath of resignation. "Why?"

"Because nothing about this conversation—which *you* initiated—is professional in nature." He deliberately let his gaze drop to the sapphire sparkling against her alabaster skin, then took a long, appreciative look at the swell of her breasts.

"You're insatiable," she said with a definite note of disgust.

He smiled. "Most women like that about me."

"I'm not most women."

"We'll see about that, won't we?"

The car slowed to a stop in front of the gilded entrance to the Waldorf Astoria. A red carpet covered the walkway from the curb to the gold-trimmed doors, flanked on either side by a mob of paparazzi too numerous to count.

"Miss Drake and Mr. Andrade, we've arrived," the driver said.

"Thank God. I need to get out of this car." Diana reached for the door handle, but her violet eyes grew wide. "Oh, wait. I almost forgot."

She opened her tiny, beaded clutch, removed a Drake-blue box and popped it open. The black diamond cuff links from the photo shoot glittered in the velvety darkness.

She handed them to Franco as the driver climbed out of the car. "Put these on. Quickly."

He slid one into place on his shirt cuff, but left the other in the palm of his hand.

"What are you doing? Hurry." Diana was borderline panicking. The back door clicked open, and the driver extended his hand toward her and waited.

"Go ahead, it's showtime." Franco loosened his tie and winked. "Trust me, Wildfire."

She stretched one foot out of the car, aimed a dazzling smile at the waiting photographers and muttered under her breath, "You realize that's asking the impossible."

Franco gathered the soft chiffon hem of her gown and helped her out of the limo. They stepped from the quiet confines of the car into a frenzy of clicking camera shutters and blinding light.

He dropped a kiss on Diana's bare shoulder and made a show of fastening the second cuff link in place. A collective gasp rose from the assembled crowd of spectators.

He lowered his lips to Diana's ear. "I have everything under control."

I have everything under control.

Maybe if he repeated it enough times, it would be true.

The man is an evil genius.

Diana hadn't been sure what Franco had up his sleeve until she felt his lips brush against her shoulder.

The kiss caught her distinctly off guard, and as her head whipped around to look at him, she saw him fastening his cuff link. He curved his arm around her waist, murmured in her ear and she finally understood. He'd purposely delayed sliding the diamonds into position on his shirt cuff so it looked as though he was only just getting dressed, no doubt because their arrival at the gala had caught them in flagrante delicto.

The press ate it up.

Evil genius. Most definitely.

"Diana, how long have you and Franco been dating?"

"Diana, who are you wearing?"

"Look over here, Diana! Smile for the camera."

Photographers shouted things from every direction.

She didn't know where to look, so she bowed her head as Franco steered her deftly through the frenzied crowd with his hand planted protectively on the small of her back.

"What's the diamond heiress like in bed, Franco?" a paparazzo yelled.

Diana's head snapped up.

"Don't let them get to you," Franco whispered.

"I'm fine," she lied. The whole scene was madness. "But if you answer that question, I will murder you."

"A gentleman doesn't kiss and tell."

Their eyes met briefly in the chaos, and if Diana hadn't known better, she would have believed he was being serious.

Suddenly, the thought of doing this for twenty-one straight days seemed absurd. Absurd and wholly impossible.

"Good evening, Miss Drake, Mr. Andrade." The doorman nodded and swept the door open for them. "Welcome to the Waldorf Astoria."

"Gracias," Franco said. *Thank you.* He gave her waist a gentle squeeze. "Shall we, love?"

His voice rumbled through her, deliciously deep.

She swallowed. *It's all pretend. Don't fall for it. Don't fall.*

She'd told herself the same thing three years ago. A fat lot of good that had done her.

Everything was moving too fast. Even after they finally made it inside the grand black-and-white marble lobby, Diana felt as if she'd been caught up in a whirlwind. A glittering blur where everything was too big and too bright, from the mosaic floor to the grand chandelier to the beautiful man standing beside her.

"Miss Drake and Mr. Andrade, I'm Beth Ross, director of Manhattan Pet Rescue. We're so pleased you could make it to our little gathering this evening."

"Ah, Beth, we wouldn't have missed it for the world," Franco said smoothly, following up his greeting with a kiss on the cheek.

Beth practically swooned.

He was so good at this it was almost frightening. If Artem had really known what he was doing, he would have made Franco the new vice president of public relations.

Say something. You're not the arm candy. He is.

"Thank you for having us. We're so pleased to be here." Diana smiled.

From the corner of her eye, she spotted someone holding up a cell phone and pointing toward her and Franco. He must have seen it too, because he deftly wrapped his arm around her waist and rested his palm languidly on her hip. Without even realizing it, she burrowed into him.

Beth sighed. "You two are every bit as beautiful

as your advertising campaign. It's all anyone can talk about."

"So we've heard." Diana forced a smile.

"Our party is located upstairs in the Starlight Ballroom. I've come to escort you up there, and if you don't mind, we'd love to snap a few pictures of you with some of the animals we have up for adoption later this evening."

Diana stiffened. "Um…"

Franco gave her hipbone a subtle squeeze. "We'd be happy to. We're big animal lovers, obviously."

We're big animal lovers.

We.

Diana blinked. Franco seemed to be staring at her, waiting for her to say something. "Oh, yes. Huge animal lovers."

They moved from the glitzy, gold lobby into a darkly intimate corridor walled in burgundy velvet. Beth pushed a button to summon an elevator.

"That doesn't surprise me a bit," she said. "I just knew you must be animal lovers. Drake Diamonds has always been one of our biggest supporters. And, of course, both of you are legendary in the horse world."

The elevator doors swished open, and the three of them stepped inside.

"Diana has a beautiful black Hanoverian. Tell Beth about Diamond, love." Franco looked at her expectantly.

Diana felt as though she'd been slapped.

She opened her mouth to say something, anything, but she couldn't seem capable of making a sound.

"Are you all right, dear? You've gone awfully pale." Beth eyed her with concern.

"I just… I…" It was no use. She couldn't talk about Diamond. Not now.

For six months, she'd managed to avoid discussing her beloved horse's death with anyone. Not even her brothers. She knew she probably should, but she couldn't. It just hurt too much. And after so much silence, the words wouldn't come.

"She's a bit claustrophobic," Franco said.

Another lie. Diana was beginning to lose track of them all.

"Oh, I'm so sorry." Beth's hand fluttered to her throat. "I didn't realize. We should have taken the stairs."

"It's fine." Franco's voice was like syrup. Soothing. "We're almost there, darling."

The elevator doors slid open.

Diana burrowed into Franco as he half carried her to the entrance to the ballroom. She couldn't remember leaning against him in the first place.

Breathe in, breathe out. You're fine.

She took a deep inhale and straightened her spine, smiled. "So sorry. I'm okay. Really."

Her heart pounded against her rib cage. She desperately wished she were back at Dalton's apartment, watching bad reality television and curled up under a blanket on the sofa.

Don't think about Diamond. Don't blow this. Say something.

She glanced up at the stained-glass ceiling strung with twinkling lights. "Look how beautiful everything is."

Beth nodded her agreement and launched into a description of all the work that had gone into putting together the gala, a large part of which had been funded by Drake Diamonds. Diana smiled and nodded, as did Franco, although at times she could see him watching her with what felt like too much interest.

She was dying to tell him he was laying it on a little

thick. They were supposed to be dating, not engaged, for crying out loud. Besides, she'd shaken off the worst of her panic.

She was fine. She just hadn't expected him to mention Diamond. That's all. She'd assumed that Franco had known about her accident. Apparently, he hadn't. Otherwise, he never would have brought up Diamond.

She'd been shocked, and probably a little upset. But it had passed.

He didn't need to be worried about her, and he definitely didn't need to be watching her like that. But an hour into the gala they were still shaking hands and chatting with the other animal shelter donors. She and Franco hadn't had a moment alone together.

Not that Diana was complaining.

The limousine ride had provided plenty of one-on-one time, thank you very much.

"If we could just ask you to do one last thing…" Beth guided them toward the far corner of the ballroom where guests had been taking turns posing for pictures. "Could we get those photos I mentioned before you leave?"

Diana nodded. "Absolutely."

Franco's hand made its way to the small of her back again. She was getting somewhat used to it and couldn't quite figure out if that was a bad thing or a good one.

It's nearly over. Just a few more minutes.

One night down, twenty to go. Almost.

She allowed herself a subtle, premature sigh of relief. Then she noticed a playpen filled with adorable, squirming puppies beside the photographer's tripod, and any sense of triumph she felt about her performance thus far disintegrated. She couldn't handle being around animals again. Not yet.

"Well, well. What do we have here?" Franco reached

into the playpen and gathered a tiny black puppy with a tightly curled tail into his arms.

The puppy craned its neck, stuck out its miniscule pink tongue and licked the side of Franco's face. He threw his head back and laughed, which only seemed to encourage the sweet little dog. It scrambled up Franco's chest and showered his ear with puppy kisses.

Beth motioned for the photographer to capture the adoration on film. "Doesn't she just love you, Mr. Andrade?"

The puppy was a girl. Because of course.

Franco's charm appealed to females of all species, apparently.

Why am I not surprised?

"Come here, love." Franco reached for Diana's hand and pulled her toward him. "You've got to meet this little girl. She's a sweetheart."

"No, it's okay. You keep her." She tried to wave him off, but it was impossible. Before she knew what was happening, she had a puppy in her arms and flashbulbs were going off again.

"That's Lulu. She's a little pug mix."

"Franco's right. She's definitely a sweetheart." Diana gazed down at the squirming dog.

Before her brother Dalton got married and moved to Delamotte, he'd tried talking her into getting a dog on multiple occasions. At first she'd thought he was joking. Dalton didn't even like dogs. Or so she'd thought. Apparently that had changed when he met the princess. Then he'd practically become some sort of animal matchmaker and kept encouraging Diana to adopt a pet.

What had gotten into her brothers? Both of them had turned into different people over the course of the past year. Sometimes it felt like the entire world was moving forward, full speed ahead, while Diana stood completely still.

Everything was changing. Everything and everyone.

It didn't use to be this way. From the first day she'd climbed onto the back of horse, Diana had been riding as fast as she could. She'd always thought if she rode hard enough, she'd escape the legacy Gaston Drake had built. Escape everything that it meant to be part of her family. The lies, the deceit. She'd thought she could outrun it.

Now she was back in the family fold, and she realized she hadn't outrun a thing.

She swallowed hard. How could she even consider saving a dog when she wasn't even convinced she could save herself?

"Here. You take her." She tried to hand the puppy back to Franco, but he wrapped his arms around her and kept posing for the camera.

"You three make a lovely family," Beth gushed.

That was Diana's breaking point.

The touching…the endearments…the puppy. Those things she could handle. Mostly. But the idea of being a family? She'd rather die.

"It's getting late. We should probably go."

But no one seemed to have a heard a word she said, because at the exact time that she tried to make her getaway, Franco made an announcement. "We'll take her."

Beth squealed. A few people applauded. Diana just stood there, trying to absorb what he'd said.

She searched his features, but he was still wearing that boyfriend-of-the-year expression that gave her butterflies, even though she knew without a doubt it wasn't real. "What are you talking about?"

"The puppy." He gave the tiny pup a rub behind her ears with the tip of his pointer finger.

"Franco, we can't adopt a dog together," she muttered through her smile, which was definitely beginning to fade.

"Of course we can, darling." His eyes narrowed the slightest bit.

No one else noticed because they were too busy fawning all over him.

"Franco, *sweetheart*." She shot daggers at him with her eyes.

This wasn't part of the deal. She'd agreed to pretend to date him, not coparent an animal.

Besides, she didn't want to adopt a dog. Correction: she *couldn't* adopt a dog.

A dog's lifespan was even shorter than a horse's. Much shorter. She wouldn't survive that kind of heartache. Not again. *Never* again.

Franco bowed his head to nuzzle the puppy and paused to whisper in her ear. "They're eating it up. What is your problem?"

It was the worst possible time for something to snap inside Diana, but something did. All the feelings she'd been working so hard to suppress for the past few months—the anger, the fear, the grief—came spilling out at once. She gazed up at Franco through a veil of tears as the whole world watched.

"Diamond is dead. That's my problem."

Chapter Six

A *Page Six* Exclusive Report

The rumors are true! Diamond heiress Diana Drake and polo's prince charming, Franco Andrade, are indeed a couple. Tongues have been wagging all over New York since their sultry billboard went up in Times Square. The heat between these two is too hot to be anything but genuine!

Drake and Andrade stepped out last night at Manhattan's Annual Fur Ball, where witnesses say they arrived on the heels of what was obviously a romantic tryst in the Drake Diamonds limousine. During the party, Andrade was heard calling Drake by the pet name Wildfire and couldn't keep his hands off the stunning equestrian beauty.

At the end of the evening, Drake was moved to tears when Andrade gifted her with a nine-week-old pug puppy.

Chapter Seven

Franco shifted his Jaguar into Park and swiveled his gaze to the passenger seat. "I don't suppose I can trust you to stay here and let me do the talking."

Lulu let out a piercing yip, then resumed chewing on the trim of the Jag's leather seats.

"Okay, then. Since you've made no attempt at all to hide your deviousness, you're coming with me." He scooped the tiny dog into the crook of his elbow and climbed out of the car.

"Try to refrain from gnawing on my suit if you can help it."

Lulu peered up at him with her shiny, oversize eyes as she clamped her little teeth around one of the buttons on his sleeve.

Marvelous.

Franco didn't bother reprimanding her. If the past week had taught him anything, it was that Lulu had a mind of her own. Not unlike the other headstrong female in his life…

Diana hadn't been kidding when she said she didn't want anything to do with the puppy. As far as pet parenting went, Franco was a single dad. Which would have been fine, had he not known how badly she needed the dog.

She was reeling from the loss of her horse. That much was obvious. If anyone could understand that kind of grief, Franco could.

He'd had no idea that Diamond had died. But now that he knew, things were beginning to make more sense. Diana hadn't given up riding because she had a burning desire to peddle diamonds. She was merely hiding out at the family store. She was heartbroken and afraid.

But she couldn't give up riding forever.

Could she?

"Franco." Ben Santos, the coach of the Kingsmen, strolled out of the barn and positioned himself between Franco and the practice field. "What are you doing here?"

Not exactly the greeting he was hoping for.

Franco squared his shoulders and kept on walking. Enough was enough. He needed to stop worrying so much about his fake girlfriend and focus on resurrecting his career.

"Nice to see you too, coach." He paused by the barn and waited for an invitation onto the field.

None was forthcoming.

Ben squinted into the sun and sighed. "You know you're not supposed to be here, son."

Franco's jaw clenched. He'd never liked Ben's habit of calling his players *son*. Probably because the last man who'd called Franco that had been a worthless son of a bitch.

But he'd put up with it from Ben out of respect. He wasn't in the mood to do so now, though.

Seven nights of wining and dining Diana Drake at every charity ball in Manhattan had gotten him absolutely nowhere. He had nothing to show for his efforts, other than a naughty puppy and a nagging sense that Diana was on the verge of coming apart at the seams.

Not your problem.

"I was hoping we could talk. Man to man," Franco said. Or more accurately, man to man holding tiny dog.

Lulu squirmed in his grasp, and the furrow between Ben's brows faded.

"Nice pup," he said. "This must be the one I've been reading about in all the papers."

Thus far, Lulu's puppyhood had been meticulously chronicled by every gossip rag and website Franco had ever heard of, along with a few he hadn't. Just this morning, Franco had been photographed poop-scooping outside his Tribeca apartment. He supposed he had that lovely image to look forward to in tomorrow's newspapers. Oh, joy.

He cleared his throat. "So you've been keeping up with me."

Excellent. Maybe the love charade was actually working.

"It's been kind of hard not to." Ben reached a hand toward Lulu, who promptly began nibbling on his fingers.

"The publicity should come in handy when the season starts, don't you think?" Franco's gaze drifted over the coach's shoulder to where he could see a groom going over one of the Kingsmen polo ponies with a curry comb. The horse's coat glistened like a shiny copper penny in the shadows of the barn.

Diamond is dead. That's my problem.

"Except you're not on the team, so, no." Ben shook his head.

"This has gone on long enough, don't you think? You need me. The team needs me. How long is Ellis planning on making me sweat this out?"

"You were fired. And I don't think Ellis is going to change his mind. He's furious. Frankly, I can't blame him." Ben removed his Kingsmen baseball cap and raked a hand through his hair. He sighed. "You went too far this time, son. You slept with the man's wife."

Franco pretended he hadn't heard the last sentence. If he thought about it too much, he might be tempted to tell the truth and he couldn't do that. Luc had his faults—bedding the boss's wife chief among them—but he was Franco's friend. Luc had been there for him when he needed someone most.

Franco owed Luc, and it was time to pay up.

"That's over." Franco swallowed. "I'm in love."

He waited for a lightning bolt to appear out of the sky and strike him dead.

Nothing happened. Franco just kept standing there, holding the squirming puppy and watching the horses being led toward the practice field.

He missed this. He missed spending so much time with his horses. He'd been exercising them as often as possible, but it couldn't compare with team practice, day in and day out.

Diana had to miss it, too. He knew she did.

Diamond is dead. That's my problem.

Franco felt sick every time he remembered the lost look in Diana's eyes when she'd said those words.

Her vulnerability had caught him off guard. It affected him far more than her disdain ever could. He didn't mind being hated. He deserved it, frankly. But he *did* mind seeing Diana in pain. He minded it very much.

Again, not his problem. He was here to get himself, not Diana, back in the saddle.

"In love," Ben repeated. His gaze dropped to the rich soil beneath their feet. "I'm happy to hear it. I am. But I'm afraid it's going to take more than a few pictures in the paper to convince Ellis."

Franco's jaw clenched. "What are you saying?"

But the coach didn't need to elaborate, because the field was filling up with Franco's team members. They were clearly preparing for a scrimmage because, instead of being dressed in casual practice attire, they were wearing uniforms. Franco spotted Luc, climbing on top of a sleek ebony mount. But the sight that gave Franco pause was another player. One he'd never seen before, wearing a shirt with a number situated just below his right shoulder—the number 1.

Franco's number.

"Perhaps Ellis would feel differently if you were married. Or even engaged. Something permanent, you know. But right now, it looks like a fling. To him, anyway." Ben shrugged. "Surely you understand. Try to put yourself in his shoes, son. Imagine how you'd feel if another man, a man whom you knew and trusted, hopped into bed and ravished Miss Drake."

Franco's gaze finally moved away from the player wearing his number. He stared at the coach, and a nonsensical rage swelled in his chest. A thick, black rage, which he could only attribute to the fact that he'd been replaced. "Don't talk about her that way."

Ben held up his hands. "I'm not suggesting it will happen. I'm simply urging you to try and understand where Ellis is coming from."

"This isn't about Diana." Franco took a calming inhale and reminded himself that losing his cool wasn't going to do him any favors. "It's not even about Ellis and his wife. It's about the team."

The coach gestured toward the bright-green rectangle of grass just west of the barn. "Look, son. I need to get going. We've got back-to-back scrimmages this afternoon."

Franco jerked his chin in the direction of the practice field. "Who's your new number 1?"

Ben sighed. "Don't, Franco."

"Just tell me who's wearing my jersey, and I'll leave."

"Gustavo Anca."

"You can't be serious." Franco knew Gustavo. He was a nice enough guy, but an average player at best. Ellis was playing it safe. Too safe. "You know he won't bring in the wins."

"Yes, but he won't sleep with the owner's wife, either." The older man gave him a tight smile.

Franco's gaze flitted ever so briefly to Luc sitting atop his horse, doing a series of twisting stretches. He turned in Franco's direction, and their eyes met.

Franco looked away.

"Listen. Can I give you a piece of advice?"

Whatever he had to say, Franco didn't want to hear it.

"Move on. Let the other teams know you're available. Someone is bound to snap you up."

He shook his head. "Out of the question."

The Kingsmen were the best. And when Franco had worn the Kingsmen jersey, he'd been the best of the best. He'd earned his place there, and he wanted it back. His horses were there. His teammates. His heart.

Also, if the Kingsmen were already scrimmaging, it could only mean the rosters had been set for the coming season in Bridgehampton. If Franco wanted to play anywhere before autumn, he'd have to go Santa Barbara. Or even as far as Sotogrande, in Spain.

He couldn't leave. He'd made a promise to the Drakes. And for the time being, his position as the face of Drake Diamonds was the only thing paying his bills.

His hesitancy didn't have a thing to do with Diana. At least, that's what he wanted to believe.

"Think about it. Make a few calls. If another team needs a reference, have them contact me." Ben shifted from one foot to the other. "But I can only vouch for your playing. Nothing else."

"Of course." The tangle of fury inside Franco grew into something dark and terrible. He clamped his mouth shut.

"It was good to see you, but please understand. The situation isn't temporary." His coach gave him a sad smile. "It's permanent."

"Miss Drake, you have a visitor." The doorman's voice crackled through the intercom of Diana's borrowed apartment. "Mr. Andrade is on his way up."

Diana's hand flew to the Talk button. "Wait. What? *Why?*"

Franco was here? Now?

There had to be some sort of mistake. They weren't scheduled to arrive at the Harry Winston party for another hour and a half. She wasn't even dressed yet. Besides, she'd given the driver strict instructions to pick her up first. She didn't need Franco anywhere near her apartment. Their lives were already far more intertwined than she'd ever anticipated.

She'd even talked to him about Diamond. Briefly, but still. It had been the closest she'd come to admitting to anyone that she was having trouble moving past her accident. It had also been the first time she'd said Diamond's name out loud since her fall.

She'd spent the intervening days since the Fur Ball carefully shoring up the wall around her heart again. She went through the motions with Franco, speaking to him as little possible. He was the last person she should be confiding in. His casual reference to Diamond had caught her off guard. She'd had a moment of weakness.

It wouldn't happen again.

Even if the sight of him with that adorable puppy in his arms made her weak in the knees…she was only human, after all.

The doorman's voice crackled through the intercom. "I assumed it was acceptable, given the nature of your relationship, that I could go ahead and send Mr. Andrade up."

The nature of their relationship. Hysterical laughter bubbled up Diana's throat.

She swallowed it down. "It's fine. Thank you."

She took a deep breath and told herself to get a grip. She couldn't reprimand the doorman for sending the purported love of her life up to see her, could she?

The building that housed Dalton's apartment was one of the most exclusive addresses in Lenox Hill. She wholeheartedly doubted the doorman would be indiscreet. But the press was always looking for a scoop. The last thing she and Franco needed was a headline claiming she'd turned him away from her door.

Diana shook her head. Not she and Franco. She and Artem. The Drakes were the ones who were on the same team. Franco was just an accessory.

A dashing, dangerous accessory.

Three solid knocks pounded on the door and echoed

through the apartment. Diana tightened the belt of her satin bathrobe and opened the door.

"Franco, what a pleasant surprise," she said with forced enthusiasm.

"Diana," he said flatly.

That was it. No loving endearment. No scandalous quip about her state of near undress. Just her name.

She motioned for him to come inside and shut the door.

Her smile faded as she turned to face him. There was no reason for pretense when they were alone together. Although, now that she thought about it, this was the first time since embarking on their charade that they'd been alone. *Truly* alone. Everywhere they went, they were surrounded by drivers, photographers, doormen.

A nonsensical shiver passed through her as she looked up at him. His eyes seemed darker than usual, his expression grim.

"What are you doing here?"

Had something happened? Had word gotten out that they'd been faking their love affair? Surely not. Artem would have said something. She'd talked to him on the phone only moments ago, and everything had seemed fine.

"We have a date this evening, do we not?" His words were clipped. Formal.

Diana never thought she'd miss his sexually charged smile and smug attitude, but she kind of did. At least that version of Franco was somewhat predictable. This new persona seemed quite the opposite.

"We do." She nodded and waited for him to ogle her. She was wearing a white satin minibathrobe, for crying out loud.

He just stood there in his impeccably cut tuxedo with

his arms crossed. "Where are we going tonight, anyway?"

"To a party at Harry Winston."

"The jewelry store?" He frowned. "Isn't Harry Winston a direct competitor of Drake Diamonds?"

"Yes, but the Lambertis are going to be there."

"Who?" he asked blithely.

Seriously? They'd been over this about a million times. "Carla and Don Lamberti. They own the diamond, remember? *The* diamond."

"Right." His gaze strayed to her creamy satin bathrobe. Finally. "Shouldn't you be getting dressed?"

"I *was*. Until you knocked on my door." This wasn't the night for Franco to go rogue. Absolutely not. "What's with you tonight? Is something wrong? Why are you even here?"

His eyes flashed. Something most definitely wasn't right. "You're my girlfriend." He used exaggerated air quotes around the word *girlfriend*. "Why shouldn't I be here?"

"Because the car was supposed to pick me up first, and then we were going to collect you in Tribeca. That's why."

He eyed her with an intensity that made her feel warm and delicious, like she'd been sipping red wine. "I'm tired of following orders, Diana. Surely I'm not expecting too much if I want to make my own decision regarding transportation to a party."

"Um…"

"A real couple wouldn't be picked up at two separate locations. Real lovers would be in bed until the moment it was time to leave. Real lovers would, at the very least, be in the same godforsaken apartment." An angry muscle twitched in his jaw. Diana couldn't seem to look away from it. "We need this to look real. *I* need it to look real."

She'd never seen Franco this serious before. It shouldn't have been nearly as arousing as it was. Especially on a night as important as this one.

Diana nodded and licked her lips. "Of course."

She hadn't realized he'd cared so much about either the company or the diamond. Wasn't this whole lovey-dovey act just a paycheck for him? A way to get a little publicity for the Kingsmen?

Why *did* he care so much?

She realized she didn't actually know why he'd agreed to participate in their grand charade. Artem had said something about Franco changing his image, but she hadn't pressed for details. She just wanted to get through their twenty-one days together as quickly and painlessly as possible.

Franco prowled through her living room with the dangerous grace of a panther. "Where's your liquor cabinet? I need something to pass the time while you're getting ready."

Clearly this wasn't the moment for a heart-to-heart.

She crossed the living room, strode into the kitchen and pulled a bottle of the Scotch that Dalton favored from one of the cabinets. She set it on the counter along with a Waterford highball glass. "Will this do?"

Franco arched a brow. "It'll work."

"Good. Help yourself." She watched as he poured a generous amount and then downed it in a single swallow.

He eyed her as he picked up the bottle again. "Is there a problem, or are you going to finish getting dressed?"

Alarm bells were going off in every corner of her mind. Franco was definitely upset about something. She should call Artem and cancel before Franco polished off the rest of Dalton's Scotch.

But that wasn't an option. Not tonight, when they were

finally going to come face-to-face with the Lambertis. Their 1,100-carat diamond was the sole reason she was in this farce of a relationship.

She took a deep inhale and pasted on a smile. "No problem at all."

Not yet, anyway.

Chapter Eight

Diana held her breath as they climbed into the Drake limousine, hoping against hope that Franco's strange, dark mood would go unnoticed by everyone at the gala.

She kept waiting for him to slip back into his ordinary, devil-may-care persona, but somehow it never happened. They made the short trip to Harry Winston in tense silence, and for the first time, the strained, quiet ride seemed to be Franco's choice rather than hers.

She kept trying to make conversation and loosen him up, but nothing worked. She was beginning to realize how badly she'd behaved toward him over the course of the past week. *This must be how he feels every night.*

She shouldn't feel guilty. She absolutely shouldn't. This wasn't a real date. Not one of the past seven nights had been real. It had been business. All of it.

It needs to look real. I need it to look real.

As the car pulled up to the glittering Harry Winston

storefront at the corner of 5th Avenue and 57th Street—
just a stone's throw from Drake Diamonds—she turned
toward Franco.

"Are you sure you're ready for this?" she asked.

He met her gaze. The slight darkening of his irises was
the only outward sign of the numerous shots of Scotch
he'd consumed back at her apartment. Last week she
wouldn't have known him well enough to notice such a
subtle change.

"Yes. Are you?"

She felt his voice in the pit of her stomach. "Yes."

*There's still time to back out. Artem will be inside. Let
him charm the socks off the Lambertis.*

But making sure the owners of the diamond chose
to work with Drake Diamonds was her responsibility.
Not her brother's. And considering it was pretty much
her *only* responsibility, she shouldn't be passing it off
to Artem.

She'd already survived a week as Franco's faux love
interest. Surely they could pull this off for another four-
teen days. Franco would get himself together once they
were in public. He'd be his usual, charming self.

He had to.

But even walking past the mob of paparazzi gathered
in front of the arched entrance and gold-trimmed gate
at Harry Winston's storefront felt different. Franco felt
stiff beside her.

Diana missed the warmth of his hand on the small of
her back. She missed his playful innuendo. God, what
was happening to her? She hadn't actually enjoyed spending time with him.

Because that just wasn't possible.

The moment they crossed the threshold, Artem and
Ophelia strode straight toward them. When her brother

first told her they were coming, Diana had been filled with relief. Tonight was important. She could use all the reinforcements she could get. Now she wished he wasn't here to witness what suddenly felt like a huge disaster in the making.

"Diana." Artem kissed her on the cheek, then turned to shake Franco's hand. "Franco, good to see you."

The two men exchanged pleasantries while Diana greeted Ophelia. Dressed in a floor-length tulle gown, her sister-in-law looked every inch like the ballerina she'd been before taking the helm of the design department of Drake Diamonds. The diamond tiara Artem had given her as an engagement present was intricately interwoven into her upswept hair.

"You look stunning," Diana whispered as she embraced the other woman.

"Thank you, but my God. Look at yourself. You're glowing." Ophelia grinned. "That sapphire suits you."

Diana touched the deep blue stone hanging from the diamond and platinum garland around her neck. She'd worn it every night she'd been out with Franco as an homage to their billboard. "Well, don't get used to it. I doubt my brother is going to let me keep it once this is all over."

"He won't have to, remember? He won't be your boss anymore." Ophelia winked and whispered, "Girl power!"

Diana's stomach did a nervous flip. *Powerful* was the last thing she felt at the moment.

Franco bowed his head and murmured in her ear, "I'm going to fetch some champagne. I'll be right back." He was gone before she could say a word.

Artem frowned after him. "What's wrong with your boyfriend?"

Diana cast him a meaningful glance. *He's not my boyfriend.*

"Sis, I'm being serious. What's wrong with Franco?" Artem murmured.

So much for Franco's somber mood going unnoticed.

"He's fine, Artem. He's doing a wonderful job, as usual." Since when did she jump to Franco Andrade's defense?

"Really? Because he seems a little tense. You're sure he's all right?"

Ophelia looped her arm through her husband's. "Artem, leave Diana alone. She's perfectly capable of doing her job."

Thank God for sisters-in-law.

"I never insinuated she wasn't." Artem gave Diana's shoulder an affection little bump with his own. "My concern is about Andrade. He's letting this whole mess with the Kingsmen get to him."

Diana blinked. "What mess with the Kingsmen?"

"The fact that he's been dropped from the team. I'm guessing by his mood that he hasn't been reinstated yet. But I'm sure you know more about it than I do." Artem shrugged.

Franco had been *fired*?

So that's why he'd signed on with Drake Diamonds. He had as much to gain from their pretend courtship as she did.

But he was one of the best polo players in the world. Why would the Kingsmen let him go? It didn't make sense. She stared at him across the room and wondered what other secrets he was keeping.

Whatever the case, she wasn't about to tell Artem that she didn't have a clue Franco had been cut. This seemed like the sort of thing his girlfriend should know. Even a fake girlfriend.

"He's fine." She forced a smile. Doing so was becoming alarmingly easy. She probably shouldn't be so good at lying. "Really."

"How is it we're here, anyway? I feel like we've breached enemy territory," Ophelia whispered.

Diana looked around at the opulent surroundings—pale gray walls, black-and-white art deco tile floor, cut crystal vases overflowing with white hydrangeas—and tried not to be too impressed. She'd never set foot in Harry Winston before. As far as she knew, no Drake ever had. Their father was probably rolling in his grave.

"We were invited. All the high-end jewelers in the city are here. It's a power move on Harry Winston's part. I think it's their strategy to show the Lambertis that Harry Winston is the obvious choice to cut the diamond. It's bold to invite all your competitors. Confident. You have to admire it."

"Well, I don't." Diana rolled her eyes. "When you put things that way, the invitation is insulting. How dare they insinuate Drake Diamonds isn't good enough? We're the best in the world."

Artem winked at her. "My sister, a CEO in the making."

Franco returned to their group carrying two champagne flutes and offered them to Diana and Ophelia. "Ladies."

"Thank you," Ophelia said.

Diana reached for a glass and took a fortifying sip of bubbly. It was time to make her move.

She wasn't about to let the Lambertis be swayed by Harry Winston. If the egotistical power players behind this party thought she was intimidated, they were sorely mistaken. Drake Diamonds was about to totally steal the show.

We need this to look real.

She stole a glance at Franco and took another gulp of liquid courage. Someone needed to make it look real, and clearly it wasn't going to be him for once.

She moved closer to him, slipped her hand languidly around his waist and let her fingertips rest on his hip.

His champagne flute paused halfway to his lips. He glanced at her, and she let her hand drift lower until she was caressing his backside right there in Harry Winston in front of all of New York's diamond elite.

Franco cleared his throat and took a healthy gulp of champagne.

Another couple joined their small group. Artem introduced them, but their names didn't register with Diana. Her heart had begun to pound hard against her rib cage. All her concentration was centered on the feel of Franco's muscular frame beneath the palm of her hand.

"What are you doing?" he whispered.

"I'm doing exactly what you wanted. I'm making it look real." Her gaze drifted to his mouth.

He stared down at her, and the thunder in his gaze unnerved her. "This is a dangerous game you're playing, Diana. And in case you haven't noticed, I'm not in the mood for games."

She handed off her champagne flute to a waiter passing by with a silver tray. "Come with me."

"We're in the middle of a conversation." He shot a meaningful glance at Artem, Ophelia and the others.

"They won't even miss us, babe." She slid her arm through his and tugged him away.

They ended up in a darkened showroom just around the corner from the party. The only light in the room came from illuminated display cases full of gemstones and platinum. Diamonds sparkled around them like stars against the night sky.

"*Babe?* Really?" Franco arched a brow. "Why don't you just call me *honey bun*? Or *boo*?"

He could make fun of her all he wanted. At least she was trying. "You're blowing it out there. You realize that, don't you?"

A muscle flexed in his jaw. He looked as lethal as she'd ever seen him. "You're exaggerating. It's fine."

"Fine isn't good enough. Not tonight. You said so yourself." She couldn't let his icy composure get to her. Not now. "Talk to me, Franco. What has gotten into you? Did you have a bad day on the polo field or something? Did your polo pony trip over your massive ego?"

She crossed her arms and waited for him to admit the truth.

He raked a hand through his hair, and when he met her gaze, his dark eyes went soulful all of a sudden. If Diana had been looking at anyone else, she would have described his expression as broken. But that word was so wholly at odds with everything she knew about Franco, she was having trouble wrapping her head around it.

"I didn't ride today," he said quietly. "Nor have I ridden for the past month. So, no. My pony did not, in fact, trip over my massive ego."

"I know. Artem just told me." Her voice was colder than she'd intended.

She wasn't sure why she was so angry all of a sudden. She'd been the one to insist they keep things professional. And now was definitely not the time or place to discuss the fact that he was no longer playing polo.

But she couldn't seem to stop herself. The emotions she'd been grappling with since Artem so casually mentioned Franco was no longer playing with the Kingsmen felt too much like betrayal. Which didn't even make sense. Not that it mattered, though, because words were coming out of her mouth faster than she could think.

"Why didn't you say something? Why didn't you tell me?" The last thing she wanted was for him to know she cared, but the tremor in her voice was a dead giveaway.

He looked at her, long and hard, until her breath went shallow. He was so beautiful. A dark and elegant mystery.

Sometimes when she let her guard down and caught a glimpse of him standing beside her, she understood why she'd chosen him all those years ago. And despite the humiliation that had followed, she would have chosen him all over again.

"You didn't ask," he finally said.

She gave her head a tiny shake. "But…"

"But what?" he prompted.

He was going to make her say it, wasn't he? He was forcing her to go there. Again.

She inhaled a shaky breath. "But I told you about Diamond."

Their eyes met and held.

Tears blurred Diana's vision, until the diamonds around them shimmered like rain. Something moved in the periphery. She wiped a tear from her eye, and realized someone was coming.

Her breath caught in her throat.

Carla and Don Lamberti were walking straight toward them. Diana could see them directly over Franco's shoulder. Panic welled up in her chest.

The Lambertis couldn't find them like this. They most definitely couldn't see her crying. She was supposed to be in love.

In love.

For once, the thought didn't make her physically ill.

"Kiss me," she whispered.

Franco's eyes glittered fiercely in the shadows, drawing her in, pulling her toward something she couldn't quite identify. Something dark and familiar. "Diana..."

There was an ache in the way he said her name. It caught her off guard, scraped her insides.

A strange yearning wound its way through her as she reached for the smooth satin lapels of his tuxedo and balled them in her fists.

What was she doing?

"I said kiss me." She swallowed. Hard. "Now."

Franco's gaze dropped to her lips, and suddenly his chiseled face was far too close to hers. Her heart felt like it would pound right out of her chest, and she realized she was touching him, sliding her fingers through his dark hair.

She heard a noise that couldn't possibly have come from her own mouth, except somehow it had. A tremulous whimper of anticipation.

You'll regret this.

Just like last time.

Franco took her jaw in his hand and ran the pad of his thumb over her bottom lip as his eyes burned into her. His other hand slid languidly up her bare back until his fingertips found their way into her hair. He gave a gentle yet insistent tug at the base of her chignon, until her head tipped back and his mouth was perfectly poised over hers.

She felt dizzy. Disoriented. The air seemed too thick, the diamonds around them too bright. As her eyes drifted shut, she tried to remind herself of why this was happening. This wasn't fate or destiny or some misguided romantic notion.

She'd chosen it. She was in control.

It doesn't mean anything.

It doesn't.

Franco's mouth came down on hers, hot and wanting. Every bone in her body went liquid. Warmth coursed through her and, with it, remembrance.

Then there was no more thinking. No more denial. No more lying.

Not even to herself.

This kiss was different than their last.

Franco thought he'd been prepared for it. After all, this wasn't the first time his lips had touched Diana Drake's. They'd been down this road before. He remembered the taste of her, the feel of her, the soft, kittenish noise she made right when she was on the verge of surrender. These were the memories that tormented him as he'd lain awake the past seven nights until, at last, he'd fallen asleep and dreamed of a hot summer night long gone by.

But now that the past had been resurrected, he realized how wrong he'd been. A lifetime wouldn't have prepared him for a kiss like this one.

Where there'd once been a girlish innocence, Franco found womanly desire. Kissing Diana was like trying to capture light in his hands. He was wonderstruck, and rather than finding satisfaction in the warm, wet heat of her mouth, he felt an ache for her that grew sharper. More insistent. Just...

More.

He actually groaned the word aloud against the impossible softness of lips and before he knew what he was doing, he found himself pressing her against the cold glass of a nearby jewelry display case as his fingertips slid to her wrists and circled them like bracelets.

What the hell was happening?

This wasn't just different than the last time he'd kissed

Diana. It was different from any kiss Franco had experienced before.

Ever.

He pulled back for a blazing, breathless moment to look at her. He searched her face for some kind of indication he wasn't alone in this. He wanted her to feel it too—this bewildering connection that grabbed him by the throat and refused to let go. Needed her to feel it.

She gazed back at him through eyes darkened by desire. Her irises were the color of deep Russian amethysts. Rich and rare. And he knew he wasn't imagining things.

"Franco," she whispered in a voice he'd never heard her use before. One that nearly brought him to his knees. "I..."

Somewhere behind him, he heard the clearing of a throat followed by an apology. "Pardon us. We didn't realize anyone was here."

Not now.

Franco closed his eyes, desperate not to break whatever strange spell had swallowed them up. But as his pulse roared in his ears, he was agonizingly aware of Diana's wrists slipping from his grasp. And in the moment that followed, there was nothing but deep blue silence.

He opened his eyes and focused on the glittering sapphire around her neck rather than turning around. He needed a moment to collect himself as the truth came into focus.

"Mr. and Mrs. Lamberti." Diana moved away from him in a swish of tulle and pretense. "We apologize. Stay, please."

It had been an act. All of it. The caresses. The tears. The kiss.

He took a steadying inhale and adjusted his bow tie as he slowly turned around.

"Mr. Andrade, we'd know your face anywhere." A woman—Mrs. Lamberti, he presumed—offered her hand.

He gave it a polite shake, but he couldn't seem to make himself focus on her face. He couldn't tear his gaze away from Diana, speaking and moving about as if she'd orchestrated the entire episode.

Probably because she had.

"Franco, darling. The Lambertis are the owners of the diamond I've been telling you about." Diana turned toward him, but didn't quite meet his gaze.

Look at me, damn it.

"It's a pleasure to meet you both," he said.

"The pleasure is ours. Everywhere we turn, we see photos of the two of you. And now here you are, as real as can be." Mr. Lamberti laughed.

"Real. That's us. Isn't it darling?" Franco reached for Diana's hand, turned it over and pressed a tender kiss to the inside of her wrist.

Her pulse thundered against his lips, but it brought him little satisfaction. He no longer knew what to believe.

How had he let himself be fool enough to fall for any of this charade?

"It's nice to see a couple so in love." Mrs. Lamberti brought her hand to her throat. "Romance is a rarity these days, I'm afraid."

"I couldn't agree more." Franco gave Diana's waist a tiny squeeze.

Diana let out a tiny laugh. He'd been around her long enough now to know it was forced, but the Lambertis didn't appear to notice.

They continued making small talk about their diamond as Diana's gaze flitted toward his. At last. Franco saw an unmistakable hint of yearning in the violet depths of her eyes. He knew better than to believe in it, but it made his chest ache all the same.

"Wait until you see it." Mr. Lamberti shook his head. "It's a sight to behold."

"I hope I do get to see it someday," Diana said. "Sooner rather than later."

Good girl.

She was going in for the kill, as she should. That baseball-sized rock was the reason they were here, after all. Another polo player was wearing Franco's jersey, and the prospect of keeping up the charade alongside Diana suddenly seemed tortuous at best.

But he'd be damned if it was all for nothing.

"We'll be making an announcement about the diamond tomorrow, and I think you'll be pleased." Mrs. Lamberti reached to give Diana's arm a pat. "Off the record, of course."

Diana beamed. "My lips are sealed."

Mr. Lamberti winked. "In the meantime, we should be getting back to the party."

"It was lovely to meet you both," Diana said.

Franco murmured his agreement and bid the couple farewell.

The moment they were gone, he stepped away from Diana. He needed distance between them. Space for all the lies they'd both been spinning.

"Did you hear that?" she whispered, eyes ablaze. "They're making an announcement tomorrow. They're going to pick us, aren't they?"

Us.

He nodded. "I believe they are."

"We did it, Franco. We did it." She launched herself at him and threw her arms around his neck.

Franco allowed himself a bittersweet moment to savor

the feel of her body pressed against his, the soft swell of her breasts against his chest, the orchid scent of her hair as it tickled his nose.

He closed his eyes and took a deep inhale.

So intoxicating. So deceptively sweet.

He reached for her wrists and gently peeled her away.

"Franco?" She stood looking at him with her arms hanging awkwardly at her sides.

He shoved his hands in his pockets to prevent himself from touching her. "Aren't you forgetting something? We're alone now. There's no reason to touch me. No one is here to see it."

She flinched, and as she stared up at him, the look of triumph in her eyes slowly morphed into one of hurt. Her bottom lip trembled ever so slightly.

Nice touch.

"But I…"

He held up a hand to stop her. There was nothing to say. He certainly didn't need an apology. They were both adults. From the beginning, they'd both known what they were getting into.

Franco had simply forgotten for a moment. He'd fallen for the lie.

He wouldn't be making that mistake again.

"It's fine. More than fine." He shrugged one shoulder and let his gaze sweep her from top to bottom one last time before he walked away. "Smile, darling. You're getting everything you wanted."

Chapter Nine

A *Page Six* Exclusive Report

New York's own Drake Diamonds has been chosen
by the Lamberti Mining Company as the jeweler to
cut the world's largest diamond. The massive rock
was recently unearthed from a mine in Botswana
and weighs in at 1,100 carats. Rumor has it Ophelia
Drake herself will design the setting for the record-
sized diamond, which will go on display later this
month at the Metropolitan Museum of Art.

No word yet on the exact plans for the stone,
but we can't help but wonder if an engagement ring
might be in the works. Diamond heiress Diana
Drake stepped out again last night with her current flame, polo-playing hottie Franco Andrade, at
a private party at Harry Winston. Cell phone photos snapped by guests show the couple engaged in

some scorching hot PDA. Caution: viewing these pictures will have you clutching your Drake Diamonds pearls.

Chapter Ten

Pop!

The store hadn't even opened yet, and already the staff of Drake Diamonds was on its third bottle of champagne. The table in the center of the Drake-blue kitchen was piled with empty Waterford glasses and stacks upon stacks of newspapers.

Drake Diamonds and the Lamberti diamond were front-page news.

"Congratulations, Diana." Ophelia clinked her glass against Diana's and took a dainty sip of her Veuve Clicquot. "Well done."

"Thank you." Diana grinned. It felt good to succeed at something again. Although it probably should have felt better than it actually did.

Stop. You earned this. You have nothing to feel guilty about.

She swallowed and concentrated her attention on Ophelia. "Congratulations right back at you. Have you started sketching designs for the stone yet?"

Ophelia laughed. "Our involvement has only been official for about an hour, remember?"

Diana lifted a dubious brow. "So until now you've given the Lamberti diamond no thought whatsoever?"

Ophelia's expression turned sheepish. "Okay, so maybe I've been working on a few preliminary designs… just in case."

Diana laughed. "It never hurts to be prepared."

Artem's voice boomed over the chatter in the crowded room. "Okay, everyone. The doors open in five minutes. Party time's over."

Ophelia set her glass down on the table. "I'm off, then. Duty calls."

"Something tells me your job won't be in jeopardy if you hang out a little while longer," Diana said in a mock whisper.

"I know, but I seriously can't wait to get to work on the design now that I know I'm actually going to get my hands on that diamond. I almost can't believe it's happening. It hasn't quite sunk in yet." Her eyes shone with wonder. "This is real, isn't it?"

Diana took a deep breath.

This is real, isn't it?

The memory of Franco's touch hit her hard and fast… the dance of his fingertips moving down her spine…the way his hands had circled her wrists, holding her still as he kissed her…

She was beginning to lose track of what was genuine and what wasn't.

"Believe it. It's real." She swallowed around the lump in her throat and gave Ophelia one last smile before she found herself alone in the kitchen with Artem.

Diana reached for one of the tiny cakes they kept on hand decorated to look like Drake-blue boxes and bit into it. Ah, comfort food. She could use a sugary dose of comfort right now, although she wasn't quite sure why.

You're getting everything you wanted.

Why had she felt like crying when Franco uttered those words the night before?

"Can we talk for a moment, sis?" Artem sank into one of the kitchen chairs.

"Sure." Diana sat down beside him. She was in no hurry to get back to Dalton's empty apartment. She'd rather be here, where things were celebratory.

When she'd first read the news that the Lambertis had, indeed, chosen Drake Diamonds, she'd been propped up in bed sipping her morning coffee and reading her iPad. Seeing the official press announcement hadn't given her the thrill she'd been anticipating.

If she was being honest, it almost felt like a letdown. She didn't want to examine the reasons why, and she most definitely didn't want to be alone with her thoughts. Because those thoughts kept circling back to last night.

Kissing Franco. The feel of his mouth on hers, wet and wanting. The look on his face when he spotted the Lambertis.

"You okay?" Artem looked at her, and the smile that had been plastered on his face all morning began to fade.

Diana leaned over and gave him an affectionate shoulder bump. "Of course. I'm more than okay."

But she couldn't quite bring herself to meet his gaze, so she focused instead on the table in front of them and its giant pile of newspapers. The corner of *Page Six* poked out from beneath the *New York Times*, and she caught a glimpse of the now-familiar grainy image of herself and Franco kissing.

Her throat grew tight.

She squeezed her eyes closed.

"I hope that's true, sis. I do. Because I have some concerns," Artem said.

Diana's eyes flew open. "Concerns. About what?"

He paused and seemed to be choosing his words with great care.

"You and Franco," he said at last.

She blinked. "Me and Franco?"

Artem's gaze flitted to *Page Six*. "I'm starting to wonder if this charade has gone too far."

"You can't be serious. The whole plan was your idea." She waved a hand at the empty bottles of Veuve Clicquot littering the kitchen. "And it worked. We did it, Artem."

"Yes. So far it's been a remarkable success." He nodded thoughtfully. "For the company. But some things are more important than business."

Who was his guy and what had he done with her brother? Everything they'd done for the past few weeks had been for the sake of Drake Diamonds. "What are you getting at, Artem?"

But she didn't have to ask. Deep down, she knew.

"This." He pulled the copy of *Page Six* out from beneath the *Times* and tossed it on top of the pile.

She didn't want to look at it. It hurt too much to see herself like that.

"It was just a kiss, Artem." Her brother was watching her closely, waiting for her to crack, so she forced herself to look at the photograph.

It was worse than the enormous billboard in Times Square. So much worse. Probably because this time she hadn't been acting. This time, she'd wanted Franco to take her to bed.

Her self-control was beginning to slip. Along with her

common sense. The kiss had pushed her right over the edge. It had made her forget all the reasons she despised him. Even now, she was still struggling to remember his numerous bad qualities. It was like she was suffering from some kind of hormone-induced amnesia.

Artem lifted a brow. Thank God he couldn't see inside her head. "That looks like more than *just a kiss* to me."

"As it should." She crossed her arms, leaned back in her chair and glared at him. He was pulling the overprotective brother act on her now? *Seriously?* "The whole point of our courtship is to make people believe it's real. Remember?"

"Of course I remember. And yes, I'm quite aware it was my idea. But I never said anything about kissing." He shot her a meaningful glance. "Or making out in dark corners. Where was this picture taken? Because this looks much more like a private moment than a public relations party stunt."

It took every ounce of will power Diana possessed to refrain from wadding up the paper and throwing it at him. "I can't believe what I'm hearing. For your information, the only reason I kissed him was because the Lambertis were walking straight toward us. I had to do something. I didn't want them to think Franco and I were arguing."

"Were you?" Artem raised his brows. "Arguing?"

She sighed. "No. Yes. Well, sort of."

"If there's nothing actually going on between you and Franco, what do you have to argue about?"

Diana shifted in her chair. Maybe Artem *could* see inside her head.

Of course he couldn't. Still, she should have had a dozen answers at the ready. People who weren't lovers argued all the time, didn't they?

But she couldn't seem capable of coming up with a

single viable excuse. She just sat there praying for him
to stop asking questions.

Finally, Artem put her out of her long, silent misery.
"Is there something you should tell me, Diana?"

"There's nothing going on between Franco and me.
I promise." Why did that sound like a lie when it was
the truth?

Worse, why did the truth feel so painful?

You do not *have feelings for Franco Andrade. Not
again.*

"You're a grown-up. I get that. It's just that you're my
sister. And as you so vehemently pointed out less than
two weeks ago, Franco is a man whore." Artem looked
pointedly at the photo splashed across *Page Six.* "I'm
starting to think this whole farce was a really bad idea."

"Look, I appreciate the concern. But I can handle myself around Franco. The kiss was my idea, and it meant
nothing." It wasn't supposed to, anyway. "End of story."

She stood and began clearing away the dirty champagne flutes and tossing the empty Veuve Clicquot bottles into the recycling bin. She couldn't just sit there and
talk about this anymore.

"Got it." To Diana's great relief, Artem rose from his
chair and headed toward the hallway.

But he lingered in the doorway for a last word on the
subject. "You know, we can stop this right now. You've
proven your point. You have a lot to offer Drake Diamonds. I was wrong to put you in this position."

"What?" She turned to face him.

Surely she hadn't heard him right.

He nodded and gave her a bittersweet smile. "I was
wrong. And I'm sorry. Say the word, and your fake relationship with Franco can end in a spectacular or not-so-
spectacular fake breakup. Your choice."

Her choice.

But she didn't have a choice. Not really.

A week ago, she would have given anything to get Franco out of her life. Now it didn't seem right. Not when she'd gotten what she needed out of the deal and Franco apparently hadn't.

Smile, darling, you're getting everything you wanted.

He'd played his part, and she owed it to him to play hers. Like or not, they were stuck together until the gala.

"You know that's not possible, Artem. We haven't even finalized things with the Lambertis. They could take their diamond and hightail it over to Harry Winston."

"I know they could. I'm beginning to wonder if it would really be so awful if they did." Artem sighed, and she could tell just by the look on his face that he was thinking about the photo again. *Page Six*. The kiss. "Is it really worth all of this? Is anything?"

"Absolutely." She nodded, but a tiny part of her wondered if he might be right. "You're making a big deal out of nothing. I promise."

It was too late for doubts. She'd made her bed, and now she had to lie in it. Preferably alone.

Liar.

Artem nodded and looked slightly relieved, which was still a good deal more relieved than Diana actually felt. "I suppose I should know better than to believe everything I read in the papers, right?"

She picked up the copy of *Page Six*, intent on burying it at the bottom of the recycling bin. It trembled in her hand.

She tossed it back onto the surface of the table and crossed her arms. "Exactly."

How was she going to survive until the gala? She

dreaded seeing Franco later. Now that he seemed intent on not kissing her again, it was all she could think about.

Even worse, how could she look herself in the mirror when she could barely look her brother in the eye?

Franco gave the white ball a brutal whack with his mallet and watched it soar through the grass right between the goal posts at the far end of the practice field on his Hamptons property.

Another meaningless score.

His efforts didn't count when he was the only player on the field. But he needed to be here, as much for his ponies as for himself. They needed to stay in shape. They needed to be ready, even if it was beginning to look less and less like they'd be returning to the Kingsmen.

Last night had been a reality check in more ways than one. He wasn't sure what had enraged him more—seeing his number on another player's chest or realizing Diana had asked him to kiss her purely for show.

He knew his fury was in no way rational, particularly where Diana was concerned. Their entire arrangement was based on deception. He just hadn't realized he would be the one being deceived.

But even that shouldn't have mattered. He shouldn't have cared one way or another whether Diana really wanted his mouth on hers.

And yet…he did care.

He cared far more than he ever thought he would.

I'm not yours, Mr. Andrade. Never have been, never will be.

Franco wiped sweat from his brow with his forearm, rested his mallet over his shoulder and slowed his horse to an easy canter. As he watched the mare's thick muscles move beneath the velvety surface of her coat, he thought of Diamond.

He thought about Diana's dead horse every time he rode now. He thought about the way she could barely seem to make herself say Diamond's name. He thought about her reluctance to even hold Lulu. She was afraid of getting attached to another animal. That much was obvious. Only one thing would fix that.

She needed to ride again.

Of course, getting Diana back in the saddle was the last thing he should be concerned about when he couldn't even manage to get himself back on his team.

That hadn't stopped him from dropping Lulu off at Drake Diamonds before he'd headed to the Hamptons. Artem's secretary, Mrs. Barnes, had looked at him like he was crazy when he'd handed her the puppy and asked her to give it to Diana. Maybe he *had* gone crazy. But if he'd forced the dog on Diana himself, she would have simply refused.

She needed the dog. Franco had never in his life met anyone who'd needed another living creature so much. Other than himself when he'd been a boy...

Maybe that's why he cared so much about helping Diana. Despite their vastly different upbringings, he understood her. Whether she wanted to admit it or not.

Let it go. You have enough problems of your own without adding Diana Drake's to the mix.

She didn't want his help, anyway, and that was fine. He was finished with her. As soon as the gala was over and once he had his job back, they'd never see each other again. He was practically counting the minutes.

"Andrade," someone called from the direction of the stalls where Franco's other horses were resting and munching on hay in the shade.

Franco squinted into the setting sun. As he headed off the field, he spotted a familiar figure walking toward him across the emerald-green grass.

Luc.

Franco slid out of his saddle and passed the horse's reins to one of his grooms. *"Gracias."*

It wasn't until he'd closed the distance between himself and his friend that he recognized a faint stirring in his chest. Hope. Which only emphasized how pathetic his situation was at the moment. If the Kingsmen wanted him back, the coach wouldn't send Luc. Santos would be here. Maybe even Ellis himself.

He removed his helmet and raked a hand through his dampened hair. "Luc."

"Hola, mano." Luc nodded toward the goal, where the white ball still sat in the grass. "Looking good out there."

"Thanks, man." An awkward silence settled between them. Franco cleared his throat. "How was the scrimmage yesterday?"

Luc's gaze met his. Held. "It was complete and utter shit."

"I wish I could say I was surprised. Gustavo Anca. Really? He's a six-goal player." Not that a handicap of six was bad. Plenty of world-class players were ranked as such. But Franco's handicap was eight. On an average day, Gustavo Anca wouldn't even be able to give him a run for his money. On a good day, Franco would have wiped the ground with him.

Luc nodded. "Well, it showed."

Franco said nothing. If Luc was hoping for company in his commiseration, he'd just have to be disappointed.

"Look, Franco. I came here to tell you I can't let this go on. Not anymore." Franco shook his head, but before he could audibly protest, Luc held up a hand. "I don't want to hear it. We've waited long enough. The Kingsmen are going to lose every damn game this season if we don't get you back. I'm going to Jack Ellis first thing in the morning, and I'm going to tell him the truth."

"No, you're not," Franco said through gritted teeth.

He'd made a promise, and he intended to keep it. Even if that promise had sent his life into a tailspin.

"It's not up for discussion. I don't know why I let you talk me into this in the first place." Luc shook his head and dropped his gaze to the ground.

He knew why. They both did.

"It's too late to come clean." Would Ellis even believe them if they told the truth this late in the game? Would anyone? Franco doubted it, especially in Diana's case. She'd made up her mind about him a long time ago.

But why should her opinion matter? She had nothing to do with this. Their lives had simply become so intertwined that Franco could no longer keep track of where his ended and hers began.

"I don't believe that. It's not too late. I love you like a brother. You know I do. You don't owe me a thing, Franco. You never did, and you certainly don't owe me this." Luc looked up again with red-rimmed eyes.

Why was he making this so difficult? "What's done is done. Besides, what's the point? If you tell the truth, you know what will happen."

"Yeah, I do. You'll be in, and I'll be out, which is precisely the way it should be." Luc blew out a ragged exhale. "This is bigger than the two of us, Franco. It's about the team now."

He was hitting Franco where it hurt, and he knew it. The team had always come first for Franco. Before the women, before the partying, before everything.

Until now.

Some things were bigger. Luc was family. Without Luc, Franco would never have played for the Kingsmen to begin with. He would have never even left Buenos Aires. He'd probably still be sleeping in a barn at night, or worse. He might have gone back to where he'd come from. Barrio de la Boca.

He liked to think that horses had saved him. But, in reality, it had been Luc.

He exhaled a weary sigh. "What's the point anymore? The Kingsmen can't lose you, either. If you do this, the team will suffer just as much as it already has."

"No. It won't." A horse whinnied in the distance. Luc smiled. "You're better than I am. You always were."

Franco's chest grew tight, and he had the distinct feeling they weren't talking about polo anymore.

"I came here as a courtesy, so you'd be prepared when Ellis calls you tomorrow. This is happening. Get ready." Luc turned to go.

Franco glared at the back of his head. "And if things change between now and tomorrow?"

Luc turned around. Threw his hands in the air. "What could possibly change?"

Everything.

Everything could change.

And Franco knew just how to make certain it would.

Chapter Eleven

Diana was running out of ball gowns, but that wasn't her most pressing problem at the moment. That notable distinction belonged to the problem that had four legs and a tail and had peed on her carpet three times in the past two hours.

As if Franco hadn't already made her life miserable enough, now he'd forced the puppy upon her. After Diana's awkward encounter with Artem in the Drake Diamonds kitchen, Mrs. Barnes had waltzed in and thrust the little black pug at her. She'd had no choice but to take the dog home. Now here they sat, waiting for Ophelia to show up with a new crop of evening wear.

Diana had never needed so many gowns, considering thus far she'd spent the better part of her life in riding clothes. But she'd worn nearly every fancy dress she owned over the course of her faux love affair with Franco, and she wanted to make an impression tonight. More than ever before.

The Manhattan Ballet's annual gala at Lincoln Center was one of the most important social events on the Drake Diamonds calendar. Ophelia had once been a prima ballerina at the company. Since coming to Drake Diamonds, she'd designed an entire ballet-themed jewelry collection. Naturally, the store and the Manhattan Ballet worked closely with each other.

Which meant Artem and Ophelia would be at the gala. So would the press, obviously. Coming right on the heels of the Lamberti diamond announcement, the gala would be a big deal. Huge.

It would also be the first time Diana had seen Franco since The Kiss.

But of course that had nothing to do with the fact that she wanted to look extra spectacular. Then again, maybe it did. A little.

Okay, a lot.

She wanted to torture him. First he'd had the nerve to get upset that she'd asked him to kiss her, and now he'd dropped a puppy in her lap. Who behaved like that?

Lulu let out a little yip and spun in circles, chasing her curlicue tail. The dog was cute. No doubt about it. And Diana didn't completely hate her tiny, velvet-soft ears and round little belly. If she'd had any interest in adopting a puppy, this one would definitely have been a contender.

But she wasn't ready to sign on for another heartbreak in the making. Wasn't her heart in enough jeopardy as it was?

Damn you, Franco.

"Don't get too comfortable," she said.

Lulu cocked her head, increasing her adorable quotient at least tenfold.

Ugh. "I mean it. You're not staying."

One night. That was it. Two, tops.

The doorbell rang, and Lulu scrambled toward the door in a frenzy of high-pitched barks and snorting noises. Somehow, her cuteness remained intact despite the commotion.

"Calm down, you nut." Diana scooped her up with one hand, and the puppy licked her chin.

Three nights...maybe. Then she was absolutely going back to Franco's bachelor pad.

"A puppy!" Ophelia grinned from ear to ear when Diana opened the door. "This must the one I read about in the paper."

Diana sighed. She'd almost forgotten that every detail of her life was now splashed across *Page Six*. Puppy included. "The one and only."

"She's seriously adorable. Franco has good taste in dogs. He can't be all bad." Ophelia floated through the front door of Diana's apartment with a garment bag slung over her shoulder. She might not be a professional ballerina anymore, but she still moved liked one, even with a baby strapped to her chest.

Diana rolled her eyes and returned Lulu to the floor, where she resumed chewing on a rawhide bone that was three times bigger than her own head. "I'm pretty sure even the devil himself can appreciate a cute puppy."

"The last time I checked, the devil wasn't into rescuing homeless animals." Point taken.

Ophelia tossed the garment bags across the arm of the sofa. "Enough about your charming puppy and equally charming faux boyfriend. I've come with fashion reinforcements, as you requested."

"And you brought my niece." Diana eyed the baby.

There was no denying she was precious. She had Artem's eyes and Ophelia's delicate features. Perfect in every way.

Diana just wasn't one of those women who swooned every time she saw a baby. Probably because she'd never pictured herself as a mother. Not after the nightmare of a marriage her own mother had endured.

"Here, hold her." Ophelia lifted little Emma out of the baby sling and handed her to Diana.

"Um, okay." She'd never really held Emma before. She'd oohed and aahed over her. Plenty of times. But other than the occasional, affectionate pat on the head, she hadn't actually touched her.

She was lighter than Diana had expected. Soft. Warm.

"Wow," she said as Emma took Diana's hand in her tiny grip.

"She growing like a weed, isn't she?" Ophelia beamed at her baby.

Diana studied the tender expression on her face. It wasn't altogether different from the one she usually wore when she looked at Artem. "You're completely in love with this baby, aren't you?"

"It shows?"

"You couldn't hide it if you tried." Diana rocked Emma gently from side to side until the baby's eyes drifted closed.

"It's crazy. I never pictured myself as a mother." Ophelia shrugged one of her elegant shoulders.

Diana gaped at her. "You're kidding."

"Nope. I never expected to get married, either. Your brother actually had to talk me into it." She grinned. "He can be very persuasive."

"I had no idea. You and Artem are like a dream couple."

"Things aren't always how they appear on the outside. But I don't need to tell you that." Ophelia gave her a knowing look.

Diana swallowed. "I should probably be an expert on the subject by now."

"I love your brother, and I adore Emma. I've never been so happy." And it showed. Bliss radiated from her sister-in-law's pores. "This life just isn't one I ever imagined for myself."

Maybe that's how it always worked. Maybe one day Diana would wake up and magically be ready to slip one of those legendary Drake diamonds onto her ring finger.

Doubtful, considering she was terrified of keeping the puppy currently making herself at home in Diana's borrowed apartment. "Can I ask you a question?"

"Sure. That's what sisters are for," Ophelia said.

"What changed? I mean, I know that sounds like a difficult question…"

Ophelia interrupted her with a shake of her head. "No. It's not difficult at all. It's simple, really. Love changed me."

"Love," Diana echoed, as the front-page image of herself being kissed within an inch of her life flashed before her eyes.

Please. That wasn't love. It wasn't even lust. It was pretend.

Keep telling yourself that.

"I fell in love, and that changed everything." Ophelia regarded her for a moment. "I may be way off base here, but do these questions have anything to do with Franco?"

"Hardly." Diana laughed. A little too loudly.

She couldn't ignore the truth anymore…she had a serious case of lust for the man. Everyone in New York knew she did. It was literally front-page news.

But she would have to be insane to fall in love with him. She didn't even like him. When she'd had her accident, she hadn't hit her head so hard that she lost her memory.

The day after she'd lost her virginity to Franco had been the most humiliating of her life. She'd known what she'd been getting into when she slept with him. Or thought she had, anyway.

She'd been all too aware of his reputation. Franco Andrade was a player. Not just a polo player...a *player* player. In truth, that was why she'd chosen him. His ridiculous good looks and devastating charm hadn't hurt, obviously. But mainly she'd wanted to experience sex without any looming expectation of a relationship.

She'd been twenty-two, which was more than old enough to sleep with a man. It hadn't been the sex that frightened her. It had been the idea of belonging to someone. Someone who would cheat, as her father had done for as long she could remember.

Franco had been the perfect candidate.

She'd expected hot, dirty sex. And she'd gotten it. But he'd also been tender. Unexpectedly sweet. Still, it was her own stupid fault she'd fallen for the fantasy.

She'd rather die than make that mistake again.

"Nothing at all? If you say so. There just seems to be a spark between you two," Ophelia said. "I'm pretty sure it's visible from outer space."

Diana handed the baby back to her sister-in-law. "Honestly, you sound like Artem. Did he put you up to this?"

Ophelia held Emma against her chest and rubbed her hand in soothing circles on the back of the baby's pastel pink onesie. Her brow furrowed. "No, actually. We haven't even discussed it."

Diana narrowed her gaze. "Then why are you asking me about Franco?"

"I told you. There's something special when you're together." She grinned. "Magic."

Like the kind of magic that made people believe in relationships? Marriage? *Family?* "You're seeing things. Seriously, Ophelia. You're looking at the world through love-colored glasses."

Ophelia laughed. "I don't think those are a thing."

"Trust me. They are. And you're wearing them." Diana slid closer to the garment bag and pulled it onto her lap. "A big, giant pair."

Ophelia shook her head, smiled and made cooing noises at the baby. Which pretty much proved Diana's point.

"By the way, there's only one dress in there." Ophelia nodded at the garment bag. "It's perfect for tonight. You'll look amazing in it. I was afraid if I brought more options, you wouldn't have the guts to wear this one. And you really must."

"Why am I afraid to look at it now?" Diana unzipped the bag and gasped when she got a glimpse of silver lamé fabric so luxurious that it looked like liquid platinum.

"Gorgeous, isn't it? It belonged to my grandmother. She wore it to a ballet gala herself, back in the 1940s."

Diana shook her head. "I can't borrow this. It's too special."

"Don't be silly. Of course you can. That's why I brought it." Ophelia bit her lip. "Franco is going to die when he sees you in it."

First Artem. Now Ophelia. When had everyone started believing the hype?

"Not if I kill him first," she said flatly.

The more she thought about his reaction last night, the angrier she got. How dare he call her out for doing exactly the same thing he'd been doing every night for a week?

Did he think the nicknames, the lingering glances and the way he touched her all the time didn't get to her? Newsflash: they did.

Sometimes she went home from their evenings together and her body felt so tingly, so alive that she had trouble sleeping. Last night, he'd even shown up in her dreams.

Her head spun a little just thinking about it. "I have no interest in him whatsoever."

"Yeah, you mentioned that." Ophelia smirked.

A telltale warmth crept into Diana's cheeks. "I'm serious. I'm not interested in marriage or babies, either. Certainly not with him."

"I believe you." Ophelia nodded in mock solemnity.

Even the puppy stopped chewing on her bone to stare at Diana with her buggy little eyes.

"Stop looking at me like that. Both of you. I assure you, it will be a long time before you see an engagement ring on my finger. And *if* that ever happens, the ring won't be from Franco Andrade."

He was about as far from being husband material as she was from being wife material. Diana should know...

She'd spent an embarrassing amount of time thinking it through.

Dios mío.

A little under twenty-four hours had hardly been enough time to rid Franco of the memory of kissing Diana. But the moment he set eyes on her in her liquid silver dress, everything came flooding back. The taste of her. The feel of her. The sound of her—the catch of her breath in the moment their lips came together, the tremble in her voice when she'd asked him to kiss him.

No amount of willful forgetting would erase those

memories. Certainly not while Diana was standing beside him in the lobby of Lincoln Center looking like she'd been dipped in diamonds.

A strand of emerald-cut stones had been interwoven through the satin neckline of her gown and arranged into a glittering bow just off-center from the massive sapphire draped around her neck. She looked almost too perfect to touch.

Which made Franco want to touch her all the more.

"You're staring," she said, without a trace of emotion in her voice. But the corner of her lush mouth curved into a grin that smacked of self-satisfaction.

Franco had a mind to kiss her right there on the spot.

He smiled tightly, instead. She hadn't said a word yet about the puppy stunt, which he found particularly interesting. But she was angry with him. For what, exactly, he wasn't quite sure. He was beginning to lose track of all the wrongs he'd committed, and tomorrow would be far worse. She just didn't know it yet.

He cleared his throat. "I can't seem to look away. Forgive me."

She shrugged an elegant shoulder. The row of diamonds woven through the bodice of her dress glittered under the chandelier overhead. "You're forgiven."

Forgiven.

The word and its myriad of implications hung between them.

He raised a brow. "Am I?"

He knew better than to believe it.

"It's a figure of speech. Don't read too much into it." She shifted her gaze away from him, toward the crowd assembled in the grand opera-house lobby.

Franco slipped an arm around her and led her down the red-carpeted stairs toward the party. He'd been dreading the Manhattan Ballet gala since the moment he'd woken up this morning. He'd lost his head at the Harry Winston party. He couldn't make a mistake like that again. Not now. Not when there was so much riding on his fake relationship. The Drakes may have gotten what they wanted, but Franco hadn't.

He would, though.

By tomorrow morning, everything would change.

"Diana, nice to see you. You look beautiful." Artem greeted his sister with a smile and a kiss on the cheek. When he turned toward Franco, his smile faded. "Franco."

No handshake. No small talk. Just a sharp look that felt oddly like a warning glare.

"Artem." Franco reached to shake his hand.

Something felt off, but Franco couldn't imagine why. Artem Drake should be the happiest man in Manhattan right now. His family business was front-page news. Everywhere Franco turned, people were talking about the Lamberti diamond. A few news outlets had even rechristened it the Lamberti-Drake diamond.

Would the Lambertis have even chosen Drake Diamonds if not for the pretend love affair? Franco wholeheartedly doubted it. The Lambertis had looked awfully comfortable at Harry Winston.

Until the kiss.

The kiss had been the deciding factor. Or so it seemed.

The way Franco saw things, Artem Drake should be high-fiving him right now.

Maybe he was just imagining things. After all, last night had been frustrating on every possible level. Most notably, sexually. Franco still couldn't think straight. Especially when Diana's silvery image was reflected back at him from all four walls of the mirrored room. There was simply no escaping it.

"Nice to see you again, Franco," Ophelia said warmly.

"Thank you. It's a pleasure to be here." He moved to give Ophelia a one-armed hug. Artem's gaze narrowed, and he tossed back the remainder of the champagne in his glass.

"I'm sure it is," Artem muttered under his breath.

Franco cast a questioning glance at Diana. He definitely wasn't imagining things.

"Shall we go get a drink, darling?" she said.

"Yes, let's." A drink was definitely in order. Possibly many drinks.

Once they'd taken their place in line at the bar, Franco bent to whisper in Diana's ear, doing his best not to let his gaze wander to her cleavage, barely covered by a wisp of pale gray chiffon fabric. It would have been a tall order for any man. "Are you planning on telling me what's troubling your brother? Or do I have to remain in the dark since I'm just a pretend boyfriend?"

Diana's bottom lip slipped between her teeth, a nervous habit he'd spent far too much time thinking about in recent days. After a pause, she shrugged. "I don't know what you're talking about."

"Do you really think I can't tell when you're lying?" He leaned closer, until his lips grazed the soft place just below her ear. "Because I can. I know you better than you think, Diana. Your body betrays you."

Her cheeks flared pink. "I'm going to pretend you didn't just say that."

"I'm sure you will." He looked pointedly at her mouth. "We both know how good you are at pretending."

"May I help you?" the bartender asked.

"Two glasses of Dom Pérignon, please," Franco said without taking his eyes off Diana.

"You're impossible," she said through gritted teeth.

"So you've told me." He handed her one of the two saucer-style glasses of champagne the bartender had given him. "Multiple times."

Her eyes flashed like amethysts on fire. "You've had your hands all over me for weeks, and I'm not allowed to be affected by it. But I kiss you once, and you completely lose it. You're acting like the world's biggest hypocrite."

The accusation should have angered him. At the very least, he should have been bothered by the fact that she was one hundred percent right. He was definitely acting like a hypocrite, but he couldn't seem to stop.

He'd thought the kiss was real. He'd *wanted* it to be real. He wanted that more than he'd wanted anything in a long, long time.

But he was so shocked by Diana's startling admission that he couldn't bring himself to be anything but satisfied at the moment. Satisfied and, admittedly, a little aroused.

"You like it when I touch you," he stated. It was a fact. She'd said so herself.

"No." She let out a forced laugh. "Hardly."

Yes.

Definitely.

"It's nothing to be ashamed of," he said, reaching for her with his free hand and cupping her cheek. "Would you like it if I touched you now?"

He lowered his gaze to her throat, where he could see the flutter of her pulse just above her sapphire necklace. In the depths of the gemstone, he spied a hint of his own reflection. It was like looking into a dark and dangerous mirror.

"Would *you* like it if I kissed you?" She lifted an impertinent brow.

Franco smiled in response. If she wanted to rattle him, she'd have to try harder.

"I'd like that very much. I see no need to pretend otherwise." He sipped his champagne. "I'd just prefer the kiss to be genuine."

"For your information, that kiss was more genuine than you'll ever know. Which is exactly why Artem is angry." Her gaze flitted toward her brother standing on the other side of the room.

Franco narrowed his gaze at Artem Drake. "Let me get this straight. Your brother wanted us to make everyone believe we were a couple, and now he's angry because we've done just that?"

Diana shook her head. "Not angry. Just concerned."

"About what exactly?"

She cleared her throat and stared into her champagne glass. "He thinks we've taken things too far."

Too far.

As irritating as Franco found Artem Drake's assessment of the situation, Diana's brother might be on to something.

He and Diana had crossed a line. Somewhere along the way, they'd become more to each other than business associates with a common goal.

Perhaps they'd been more than that all along. Every time Franco caught a glimpse of that massive billboard in Times Square he found himself wondering if they were somehow finishing what they'd started three years ago. Like time had been holding its breath waiting for the two of them to come together again.

He knew it was crazy. He'd never believed much in fate. Was it fate that he'd been born into the worst slum in Buenos Aires? No, fate wouldn't be so cruel. He was in control of his life. No one else.

But kissing Diana had almost been enough to make a believer out of him.

They weren't finished with each other. Not yet.

"And what about you, Diana? Do you think we've taken things too far?" He leveled his gaze at her, daring her to tell the truth.

Not far enough. Not by a long shot.

Chapter Twelve

When had things gotten so confusing?

A month ago, Diana had been bored out of her mind selling engagement rings, and now she was standing in the middle of the biggest society gala of the year being interrogated by Franco Andrade.

He shouldn't be capable of rattling her the way he did. The questions he was asking should have had easy answers.

Had they taken things too far?

Absolutely. That had happened the instant he'd fastened the sapphire around her neck. She should never have agreed to pose with him. That one photo had set things in motion that were now spinning wildly out of control.

Then she'd gone and exacerbated things by agreeing to be his pretend girlfriend. Worse yet, since she'd asked him to kiss her, she'd begun to doubt her motivation.

Did she really want to be co-CEO of Drake Diamonds? Had she ever? Or had the promotion simply been a convenient excuse to spend more time with Franco?

Surely not. She hated him. She hated everything about him.

You like it when I touch you.

Damn him and his smug self-confidence. She would have loved to prove him wrong, except she couldn't. She loved it when he touched her. The barest graze of his fingertips sent her reeling. And now she'd gone and admitted it to his face.

She lifted her chin and met his gaze. "Of course we haven't taken things too far. We're both doing our jobs. Nothing more."

"I see. And last night your job included kissing me." The corner of his mouth curved into a half grin, and all she could think about was the way that mouth had felt crashing down on hers.

"You seriously need to let that go." How could she possibly forget it when he kept bringing it up? "Besides, *you* kissed *me*."

"At your request." He lifted a brow.

Her gaze flitted to his bow tie. Looking him in the eye and pretending she didn't want to kiss him again was becoming next to impossible. "Same thing."

"Hardly. When I decide to kiss you, you'll know it. There will be no mistaking my intention." There was a sudden edge to his voice that reminded her of Artem's offer to end this farce once and for all.

Say the word, and your fake relationship with Franco can end in a spectacular or not-so-spectacular fake breakup. Your choice.

Her choice.

She'd had a choice all along, whether she wanted to admit it or not. And she'd chosen Franco. Again.

She was beginning to have the sinking feeling that she always would.

She'd tried her best to keep up her resistance. She really had. The constant onslaught of his devastating good looks paired with the unrelenting innuendo had taken its toll. But his intensity had dealt the deathblow to her defenses.

He cared. Deeply. He cared about Diamond. He cared about why she refused to ride again. That's why he'd forced her hand about the puppy. She'd known as much the moment that Mrs. Barnes had dropped the wiggling little pug into her arms.

Despite his playboy reputation and devil-may-care charm, Franco Andrade cared. He even cared about the kiss.

A girl could only take so much.

"What are you waiting for, then?" she asked, with far more confidence than she actually felt. She reminded herself that she knew exactly what she was doing. But she'd thought the same thing three years ago, hadn't she? "Decide."

A muscle tensed in Franco's jaw.

Then, in one swift motion, he gathered their champagne glasses and deposited them on a nearby tray. He took her hand and led her through the crowded lobby, toward a shadowed corridor. For once, Diana was unaware of the eyes following them everywhere they went. She didn't care who saw them. She didn't care about the Lambertis. She didn't care about the rest of the Drakes. She didn't even care about the press.

The only thing she cared about was where Franco was taking her and what would happen once they got there.

Decide, she'd implored. And decide he had.

"Come here," he groaned, and the timbre in his voice seemed to light tiny fires over every exposed surface of her skin.

He pushed through a closed door, pulling her alongside him, and suddenly they were surrounded on all sides by lush red velvet. Diana blinked into the darkness until the soft gold glow of a dimly lit stage came into focus.

He'd brought her inside the theater, and they were alone at last. In a room that typically held thousands of people. It felt strangely intimate to be surrounded by row upon row of empty seats, the silent orchestra pit and so much rich crimson. Even more so when Franco's hand slid to cradle the back of her head and his eyes burned into hers.

"This is for us and us alone. No one else." His gaze dropped to her mouth.

Diana's heart felt like it might beat right out of her chest. *You can stop this now. It's not too late.*

But it was, wasn't it? She'd all but dared him to kiss her, and she wasn't about to back down now.

She lifted her chin so that his mouth was perfectly poised over hers. "No one else."

He grazed her bottom lip with the pad of his thumb, then bent to kiss her. She expected passion. She expected frantic hunger. She expected him to crush his mouth to hers. Instead, the first deliberate touch of his lips was gentle. Tender. So reverent that she knew within moments it was a mistake.

She'd fought hard to stay numb after her fall. The less she felt, the better. So long as she kept the world at arm's length, she'd never have to relive the nightmare of what she'd been through. But tenderness—especially coming from Franco—had a way of dragging her back to life, whether or not she was ready.

"Diana," he whispered, and his voice echoed throughout the room with a ghostly elegance that made her head spin.

She'd wanted him to kiss her again since the moment their lips parted the night before. She'd craved it. But as his tongue slid into her mouth, hot and hungry, she realized she wanted more. So much more.

Was it possible to relive only part of the past? Could she sleep with him again and experience the exquisite sensation of Franco pushing inside her without the subsequent heartache?

Maybe she could. She wasn't a young, naive girl anymore. She was a grown woman. She could take him to bed with her eyes wide open this time, knowing it was purely physical and nothing more.

My choice.

He pushed her against a velvet wall and when his hands slid over the curves of her hips, she realized she was arching into him, pressing herself against the swell of his arousal. She could spend all the time in the world weighing the consequences, but clearly her body knew what it wanted. And it had made up its mind a long time ago.

Your body betrays you.

He'd been right about that, too, damn him.

"Franco," she murmured against his mouth. Was that really her voice? She scarcely recognized herself anymore.

But that only added to the thrill of the moment. She was tired of being Diana Drake. Disciplined athlete. Diamond heiress and future CEO. Perpetual good girl.

She wanted to be bad for a change.

"Yes, love?" His mouth was on her neck now, and his hands were sliding up the smooth silver satin of her dress to cup her breasts.

She was on fire, on the verge of asking him to make love to her right there in the theatre.

No. If she was going to do this, she wanted it to last. And she wanted to be the one in control. She refused to get hurt this time. She couldn't. Wouldn't.

But as she let her hands slip inside Franco's tuxedo jacket and up his solid, muscular back, she didn't much care about what happened tomorrow. How much worse could things get, anyway?

"Come home with me, Franco."

Franco half expected her to change her mind before they made it back to her apartment. If she did, it would have killed him. But he'd honor her decision, obviously.

He wanted her, though. He wanted her so much it hurt.

By the time they reached the threshold of her front door, he was harder than he'd ever been in his life. Diana gave no indication that she'd changed her mind. On the contrary, she wove her fingers through his and pulled him inside the apartment. The door hadn't even clicked shut behind them before she draped her arms around his neck and kissed him.

It was a kiss full of intention. A prelude. And damned if it didn't nearly drag him to his knees.

"Diana," he groaned into her mouth.

Everything was happening so fast. Too fast. He'd waited a long time for this. Three excruciating years. Waiting…wanting.

"Slow down, love." He needed to savor. And she needed to be adored, whether she realized it or not.

She pulled back to look at him, eyes blazing. "Just so you know, this is hate sex."

He met her gaze. Held it, until her cheeks turned a telltale shade of pink.

Keep on telling yourself that, darling.

He drew his fingertip beneath one of the slender straps of her evening gown, gave it a gentle tug and watched as it fell from her shoulder, baring one of her breasts. He didn't touch her, just drank in the sight of her—breathless, ready. Her nipple was the palest pink, as delicate as a rose petal. When it puckered under his gaze, he finally looked her in the eye.

"Hate sex. Obviously." He gave her a half smile. "What else would it be?"

"I'm serious. I loathe you." But as she said those words, she slid the other spaghetti strap off her shoulder and let her dress fall to the floor in a puddle of silver satin.

I don't believe you. He stopped short of saying it. Let her think she was the one in control. Franco knew better. "I don't care."

History swirled in the air like a lingering perfume as she stood before him, waiting. Naked, save for the dark, sparkling sapphire resting against her alabaster skin.

She was gorgeous. Perfect. More perfect than he remembered. She'd changed in the years since he'd seen her this way. There was a delicious curve to her hips that hadn't been there before, a heaviness to her breasts. He wouldn't have thought it possible for her to grow more beautiful. But she had.

Either that, or this meant more than he wanted to admit.

Hate sex. Right.

She gathered her hair until it spilled over one shoulder,

then reached behind her head to unfasten the sapphire-and-diamond necklace.

"Leave it." He put his hands on the wall on either side of her, hemming her in. "I like you like this."

"Is that so?" She reached for the fly of his tuxedo pants and slipped her hand inside.

Franco closed his eyes and groaned. He was on the verge of coming in her hand. As much as he would have liked to blame his lack of control on his recent celibacy, he knew he couldn't. It was her. Diana.

What was happening to him? To them?

"Diana," he whispered, pushing her bangs from her eyes.

He searched her gaze, and he saw no hatred there. None at all. Only desire and possibly a touch of fear. But wasn't that the way it should be? Shouldn't they both be afraid? One way or another, this would change things.

His chest felt tight. Full. As if a blazing sapphire like the one around Diana's neck had taken the place of his heart and was trying to shine its way out.

"I need you, Franco." Not want. *Need.*

"I know, darling." He grazed her plump bottom lip with the pad of his thumb. She drew it into her mouth, sucked gently on it.

Holy hell.

"Bedroom. Now." Every cell in his body was screaming for him to take her against the wall, but he wanted this to last. If they were going to go down this road together…again…he wanted to do it right this time. Diana deserved as much.

She released her hold on him and ducked beneath one of his arms. Then she sauntered toward a door at the far end of the apartment without a backward glance.

Franco followed, unfastening his bow tie as his gaze

traveled the length of her supple spine. She moved with the same feline grace that haunted his memory. He'd thought perhaps time had changed the way he remembered things, as time so often did. Surely the recollection of their night together shone brighter than the actual experience.

But he realized now that he'd been wrong. She was every bit as special as he remembered. More so, even.

He placed his hands on her waist and turned her around so she was facing him. She took a deep, shuddering inhale. The sapphire rose and fell in time with the beating of her heart.

She was more bashful now, with the bed in sight. Which made it all the more enticing when her hands found his belt. But her fingers had started trembling so badly that she couldn't unfasten the buckle.

"Let me," he said, covering her hands with his own.

He took his time undressing. He needed her to be sure. More than sure.

But once he was naked before her, her shyness fell away. She stared at his erection with hunger in her gaze until Franco couldn't wait any longer. He needed to touch her, taste her. Love her.

He hesitated as he reached for her.

This isn't love. It can't be.

The line between love and hate had never seemed so impossibly small. As his hands found the soft swell of her breasts, he had the distinct feeling they were crossing that line. He just didn't know which side they'd been on, which direction they were going.

He lowered his head to draw one of her perfect nipples into his mouth, and she gasped. An unprecedented surge of satisfaction coursed through him at the sound of her letting go. At last.

That's it, Wildfire. Let me take you there.

He teased and sucked as she buried her hands in his hair, shivering against him. He reached to part her thighs, and she let out a soft, shuddering moan. As he slipped a finger inside her, he stared down at her, fully intending to tell her they were just getting started. But when she opened her eyes, he said something altogether different.

"You have the most beautiful eyes I've ever seen. Like amethysts."

The words slipped out of his mouth before he could stop them. He loved her eyes. He always had. But this wasn't the sort of thing people said during hate sex. Even though he wasn't at all convinced that's what they were doing.

Still. This wasn't the time to turn into a romantic. If she needed to pretend this was nothing but a meaningless release, fine. He'd give her whatever she needed.

"There's a legend about amethysts, you know," she whispered, grinding against him as he moved his finger in and out.

"Tell me more."

He guided her backward until her legs collided into the bed and she fell, laughing, against the down comforter. He stretched out beside her and ran his fingertips in a leisurely trail down the perfect, porcelain softness of her belly.

Then he was poised above her with his erection pressing against her thigh, and her laughter faded away. Her eyes turned dark, serious.

"According to legend, they're magic. The ancient Romans believed amethysts could prevent drunkenness. Some still say they do."

Franco didn't believe it. Not for a minute. He felt

drunk just looking into the violet depths of those eyes. "Nonsense. You're intoxicating."

"Franco."

He really needed to stop saying such things. But he couldn't seem to stop himself.

If the circumstances had been different, he would have said more. He would have told her he'd been an idiot all those years ago. He would have admitted that this charade they'd both been dreading had been the most fun he'd had in ages. He might even have told her exactly what he thought of her breathtaking body…in terms that would have made her blush ruby red.

But circumstances weren't different. They'd been pretending for weeks. He'd just have to pretend the words weren't floating around in his consciousness, looking for a way out.

There was one thing, however, he definitely needed to say. Now, because come morning it would be too late. "Diana, there's something I need to tell you."

She shook her head as her hands found him and guided him toward her entrance. "No more words. Please. Just this."

Then he was pushing into her hot, heavenly center, and he couldn't have uttered another word if he tried.

What am I doing?

Diana's subconscious was screaming at her to stop. But for once in her life, she didn't want to listen. She didn't want to worry about what would happen tomorrow. Her entire life had been nothing but planning, practice, preparation. Where had all of that caution gotten her?

Nothing had gone as planned.

She was supposed to be on her way to the Olympics.

And here she was—in bed with Franco Andrade. Again. By her own choosing.

On some level, she'd known this was coming. She might have even known it the moment he'd first strolled into Drake Diamonds. She most definitely had known it when he'd kissed her at Harry Winston.

But the kiss had been her idea, too, hadn't it?

Oh, no.

"Oh, yes," she heard herself whisper as he slid inside her. "Yes, please."

It doesn't mean anything. It's just sex. Hate sex.

"Look at me, Wildfire. Let me see those beautiful eyes of yours." Franco's voice was tender. So tender that her heart felt like it was being ripped wide open.

She opened her eyes, and found him looking down at her with seriousness in his gaze. He kept watching her as he began to move, sliding in and out, and Diana had to bite her bottom lip to stop herself from crying out his name.

After months and months of working so hard to stay numb, to guard herself against feeling anything, she was suddenly overwhelmed with sensation. The feel of his body, warm and hard. The salty taste of his thumb in her mouth. The things he was saying—sweet things. Lovely things. Things she'd remember for a long, long time. Long after their fake relationship was over.

It was all too much. Much more than she could handle. The walls she'd been so busy constructing didn't stand a chance when he was watching her like that. Studying her. Delighting in the pleasure he was giving her.

"That's it, darling. Show me." Franco smiled down at her. It was a wicked smile. A knowing one.

He didn't just want her naked. He wanted her exposed

in every way. She could see it in the dark intent in his gaze, could feel it with each deliberate stroke.

This didn't feel like hate sex. Far from it. It felt like more. Much more.

It felt like everything.

It felt...real.

"Franco." His name tasted sweet in her mouth. Like honey. But as it fell from her lips in a broken gasp, something inside her broke along with it.

She shook her head, fighting it. She couldn't be falling for him. Not again.

It's all pretend. Just make believe.

But there was nothing make believe about his lips on her breasts as he bowed his head to kiss them. Or the liquid heat flowing through her body, dragging her under.

She arched into him, desperate, needy. He gripped her hips, holding her still as he tormented her with his mouth and his cock, with the penetrating awareness of his gaze.

This was all her doing. He knew it, and so did she.

They hadn't been destined to fall into bed together. Not then. Not now. She'd wanted him. For some nonsensical reason, she still did. Every time he touched her, every time he so much as glanced in her direction, she burned for him.

She'd made this happen. She'd seduced him. Not the other way around.

It wasn't supposed to be this way. It was supposed to be quick. Simple. But every time her climax was in reach, he slowed his movements, deliberately drawing things out. Letting her fall.

And fall.

Until everything began to shimmer like diamond dust, and she could fall no farther.

She began to tremble as her hips rose to meet his,

seeking release. Franco reached for her hands and pinned them over her head, their fingers entwined as he thrust into her. Hard. Relentless.

"My darling," he groaned, pressing his forehead against hers.

I'm not yours.

She couldn't make herself say it. Because if she did, it would feel more like a lie than any of the others she'd told in recent days. Whether she liked it or not, he held her heart in his hands. He always had, and he always would.

The realization slammed into her, and there was no use fighting it. Not now. Not when everything seemed so right. For the first time in as long as she could remember, she felt like herself again.

Because of him.

He paused and kissed her, letting her feel him pulse and throb deep inside. It was exquisite, enough to make her come undone.

"This is what you do to me, Diana." His voice was strained, pierced with truth. She felt it like an arrow through the heart. "No one else. Only you."

In the final, shimmering moment before she came apart, her gaze met his. And for the first time it didn't feel as though she was looking at the past.

In the pleasured depths of his eyes, she could see a thousand tomorrows.

Chapter Thirteen

Diana woke to a familiar buzzing sound. She blinked, disoriented. Then she turned her head and saw Franco asleep beside her—*naked*—and everything that had transpired the night before came flooding back.

They'd had sex. Hot sex. Tender sex. Every sort of sex imaginable.

She squeezed her eyes shut. Maybe it had all been a dream. A very realistic, very *naughty* dream.

The buzzing sound started again, and she sat up. Something glowed on the surface of her nightstand. Her cell phone. She squinted at it and saw Artem's name illuminated on the tiny screen.

Why was Artem calling her at this hour?

She couldn't answer the call. *Obviously.* But when she grabbed the phone to silence it, she saw that this was his third attempt to reach her.

Something was wrong.

"Hello?"

"Diana?" Artem's CEO voice was in overdrive…at six in the morning. Wonderful. "Why are you whispering?"

"I'm not," she whispered, letting her gaze travel the length of Franco's exposed torso. God, he was beautiful. *Too beautiful.*

Had her tongue really explored all those tantalizing abdominal muscles? Had she licked her way down the dark line of hair that led to his manhood?

Oh, God, she had.

She yanked one of the sheets from the foot of the bed and wrapped it around herself. She couldn't be naked while she talked to her brother. Not while the face of Drake Diamonds was sexually sated and sleeping in her bed.

"Diana, what the hell is going on?" She couldn't think of a time when she'd heard Artem so angry.

He'd found out.

Oh, no.

She slid out of bed, tiptoed out of the room and closed the door behind her. Her confusion multiplied at once when she saw heaps of feathers all over the living room. The air swirled with them, like she'd stepped straight from the bedroom into a snowfall.

A tiny black flash bounded out of one of the piles.

Lulu.

The puppy had disemboweled every pillow in sight while Diana had been in bed with Franco. Now her life was a literal mess as well as a metaphorical one. Perfect.

"Look, I can explain," she said, scooping the naughty dog into her arms.

Could she explain? Could she really?

I know I told you there was nothing going on between Franco and me, but the truth is we're sleeping together.

Slept together. Past tense. She'd simply had a bout of temporary insanity. It wouldn't happen again, obviously. It couldn't.

Hate sex. That's all it was. She'd made that very clear, and she'd stick to that story until the day she died. Admitting otherwise would be a humiliation she just couldn't bear.

"You can explain? Excellent. Because I'd really like to hear your reasoning." Artem sighed.

This was weird. And overly intimate, even by the dysfunctional Drake family standards.

"Okay…well…" She swallowed. How was she supposed to talk about her weakness for Franco's sexual charms to her *brother*? "This is a little awkward…"

Lulu burrowed into Diana's chest and started snoring. Destroying Dalton's apartment had clearly taken its toll.

"As awkward as reading about my sister's engagement in the newspaper?" Artem let out a terse exhale. "I think not."

Engagement?

Diana's heartbeat skidded to a stop.

Engagement?

Lulu gave a start and blinked her wide, round eyes.

"W-w-what are you talking about?" Diana's legs went wobbly. She tiptoed to the sofa and sank into its fluffy white cushions.

She hoped Franco was sleeping as soundly as he'd appeared. The last thing she needed was for him to walk in on this conversation.

"You and Franco are engaged to be married. It's in every newspaper in the city. It's also all over the television. Look, I know I gave you free reign as VP of public relations, but don't you think this is going a bit far?"

"Yes. I agree, but…"

TERI WILSON   *143*

"But what? The least you could have done was tell me your plans. We just talked about your relationship with Franco yesterday morning, and you never said a word about getting engaged." Artem sounded like he was on the verge of a heart attack.

Diana felt like she might be having one herself. "Calm down, Artem. It's not real."

"I know that. Obviously. But when are you going to clue everyone else in on that fact? While you're walking down the aisle?"

A jackhammer was banging away in Diana's head. She closed her eyes. Suddenly she saw herself drifting slowly down a path strewn with rose petals, wearing a white tulle gown and a sparkling diamond tiara in her hair.

What in the world?

She opened her eyes. "That's not what I mean. The announcement itself isn't real. There's been a mistake. A horrible, horrible mistake."

"Are you sure?" There wasn't a trace of relief in Artem's voice. "Because the article in the *Times* includes a joint statement from you and Franco."

"I'm positive. A statement? That's not possible. They made it up. You know how the media can be." But he'd said the *Times*, not *Page Six* or the *Daily News*.

The *New York Times* had fact checkers. It was a respectable institution that had won over a hundred Pulitzer Prizes. A paper like that didn't fabricate engagement announcements.

Now that she thought about it, the weddings section of the *Times* was famous in its own right. Society couples went to all sorts of crazy lengths to get their engagement announced on those legendary pages.

Her gaze drifted to the closed bedroom door. Ice trickled up her spine.

He wouldn't.

Would he?

No way. Franco would be just as horrified at this turn of events as she was. He wouldn't want the greater population of New York thinking he was off the market.

You and I are monogamous.

She'd actually laughed when he'd said those words less than two weeks ago. But she'd never pressed for an explanation.

This can't be happening. I can't be engaged to Franco Andrade.

Sleeping with him was one thing. Letting him slip a ring on her finger was another thing entirely.

Forget Franco. Forget Artem. Forget Drake Diamonds. This was her life, and she shouldn't be reading about it in the newspapers.

She took a calming breath and told herself there was nothing to worry about. There had to be a reasonable explanation. She didn't have a clue what that might be, but there had to be one.

But then she remembered something Franco had said the night before. Right before he'd entered her. She remembered the rare sincerity in his gaze, the gravity of his tone.

I need to tell you something.

The engagement was real, wasn't it? The statement in the *Times* had come from Franco himself. He'd even tried to warn her, and she'd refused to listen.

She hadn't wanted words. She'd wanted to feel him inside her so badly that nothing else mattered.

And now she was going to kill him.

"Artem, I have to go. I'll call you back."

She pressed End and threw her phone across the room. She glared at the closed bedroom door.

Had Franco lost his mind? They could *not* be engaged. They just couldn't. Even a fake engagement was out of the question.

Of course it's fake. He doesn't want to marry you any more than you want to marry him.

That was a good thing. A very good thing.

She wasn't sure why she had to keep reminding herself how good it was over and over and over again.

The tightness in Diana's chest intensified. She pressed the heel of her palm against her breastbone, closed her eyes and focused on her breath. She was on the verge of a full-fledged panic attack. All over an engagement that wasn't even real. If that didn't speak volumes about her attitude toward marriage, nothing would.

Breathe. Just breathe.

Maybe she was losing it over nothing. Maybe whatever Franco had wanted to tell her had nothing at all to do with the press. Maybe the *Times* wedding page had, indeed, made an unprecedented error.

She looked at the dog, because that's how low she'd sunk. She was seeking validation from a puppy. "Everyone makes mistakes. It could happen, right?"

Lulu stretched her mouth into a wide, squeaky yawn.

"You're no help at all," Diana muttered, focusing once again on the closed bedroom door.

There was only one person who could help her get to the bottom of this latest disaster, and that person didn't have four legs and a curlicue tail.

Franco slept like the dead.

He opened his eyes, then let them drift shut again. He hadn't had such a peaceful night's rest in months. He forgot all about the Kingsmen, Luc's ultimatum and the overall mess his personal life had become. It was remarkable what great sex could do for a man's state of mind. Not just great sex. Phenomenal sex. The best sex of his life.

Sex with Diana Drake.

"Franco!"

He squinted, fighting the morning light drifting through the floor to ceiling windows of Diana's bedroom.

Someone was yelling his name.

"Franco, wake up. Now." A pillow smacked his face.

He opened his eyes. "It's a little early in the morning for a pillow fight, Wildfire. But I'm game if you are."

"Of course you think that's what this is. For your information, it's not." She stood near the foot of the bed, staring daggers at him. For some ridiculous reason, she'd yanked one of the sheets off the bed and wrapped it around herself. As if Franco hadn't seen every inch of that gorgeous body. Kissed it. Worshipped it. "And I've asked you repeatedly not to call me that."

"Not last night," he said, lifting a brow and staring right back at her.

What had he missed? Because this wasn't the same Diana he'd taken to bed the night before, the same Diana who'd cried his name as he thrust inside her. It sure as hell wasn't the same Diana who'd told him how much she'd needed him as she unzipped his fly.

"I'm being serious." She tugged the bedsheet tighter around her breasts.

Franco pushed himself up to a sitting position, rested his back against the headboard and yawned. When his eyes opened, he caught Diana staring openly at his erect cock. *That's right, darling. Look your fill.* "See something you like?"

Her gaze flew upward to meet his. Franco was struck once again by just how beautiful she was, even flustered and disheveled from a night of lovemaking. He preferred her like this, actually. Fiery and flushed. He just wished she'd drop the damned sheet and climb back in bed.

"Cover yourself, please," she said primly.

"Sure. So long as I can borrow your tent." He stared pointedly at her bedsheet-turned-ballgown.

"Nice try." She let out a laugh. Laughter had to be a good sign, didn't it? "But I'll keep it, thank you very much."

Franco shrugged. "Fine. I'll stay like this, then."

Her gaze flitted once again to his arousal. If she kept looking at him like that, he might just come without even touching her. "Suit yourself. Naked or not, you have some explaining to do."

"What have I done this time?"

"I think you know." She titled her head and flashed him a rather deadly-looking smile. "My dear, darling *fiancé.*"

Fiancé.

Shit.

The engagement announcement. He'd meant to tell her about it before it hit the papers. He'd even tried to bring it up the night before, hadn't he? "So you've seen the *Times*, I presume?"

"Not yet. But Artem has. He's also seen the *Observer*, *Page Six* and the *Daily News*. It's probably the cover story on *USA TODAY*." She threw her hands up, and the sheet fell to the floor. But she'd worked herself into such a fury, she didn't even notice. "Explain yourself, Franco."

"Explain myself?" He climbed out of bed, strode toward her and picked up the pile of Egyptian cotton at her feet. Pausing ever so briefly to admire her magnificent breasts, he wrapped the sheet around her shoulders and covered her again.

Her cheeks went pink. "Thank you." For a brief second, he saw a hint of tenderness in her gaze. Then it vanished as quickly as it had appeared. "You heard me. I can't believe I even have to ask this question, but why does everyone on planet Earth suddenly think I'm going to marry you?"

He sighed and rested his hands on her shoulders, a sliver of relief working its way through him when she didn't pull away. He reminded himself the engagement was a sham. Their whole relationship was a sham. None of this should matter.

"Because I told them we're engaged."

"Oh, my God, I knew it." She began to tremble all over.

Franco slid his hands down her arms, took her hands in his and pulled her close. "No need to panic, Wildfire. It's nothing. Just part of the ruse."

A spark of something flared low in his gut. Something that felt far too much like disappointment. He'd never imagined he would one day find himself consoling a woman so blatantly horrified at the idea of being his betrothed. The fact that the woman was Diana Drake made it all the more unsettling.

She wiggled out of his grasp and began to pace around the spacious bedroom. The white bedsheet trailed behind her like the train on a wedding gown. "What were you thinking? I can't believe this."

She took a break from her tirade to regard him through narrowed eyes. For a moment, Franco thought she might slap him. Again. "Actually, I can. I don't know why I thought I could trust you. About anything."

He nearly flinched. But he knew he had no right.

As mornings after went, this one wasn't stellar. He wasn't sure what he'd expected to happen after last night.

The line between truth and lies had blurred so much he couldn't quite think straight, much less figure out whatever was happening between him and Diana. But he was certain about one thing—he'd seen the same fury in her gaze once before.

Of course he remembered what he'd said. He'd regretted the words the instant they'd slipped from his mouth.

He'd known he needed to do something dire the moment he'd woken up beside her, all those years ago. She'd looked too innocent, too beautiful with her dark hair fanned across his chest. Too damned happy.

Strangely enough, he'd felt almost happy, too. Sated. Not in a sexual way, but on a soul-deep level he hadn't experienced before. It had frightened the hell out of him.

He didn't do relationships. Never had. Never would. It wasn't in his blood. Franco had never even known who his father was, for crying out loud. As a kid, he'd watched a string of men come in and out of his mother's life. In and out of her bed. When the men were around, his mother was all smiles and laugher. Once they'd left— and they always left…eventually—the tears came. Days passed, sometimes weeks, when his mother would forget to feed him. Franco had gotten out the first chance he had. He'd been on his own since he was eleven years old. As far as he knew, his mother had never come looking for him.

He wouldn't know how to love a woman even if he wanted to. Which he didn't. If his upbringing had taught him anything, it was that self-reliance was key. He didn't want to need anyone. And he most definitely didn't want anyone needing him. Especially not a diamond heiress who'd opened her eyes three years ago and suddenly looked at him as if he'd hung the moon.

He'd done what he'd needed to do. He'd made certain she'd never look at him that way again.

Come now, Diana. We both know last night didn't mean anything. It was nice, but I prefer my women more experienced.

She'd had every right to slap him. He'd deserved worse.

"You can breathe easy. I have no intention of actually marrying you," he said.

"Good." She laughed again. Too lively. Too loud.

"Good," he repeated, sounding far harsher than he intended.

What exactly was happening?

He didn't want to hurt her. Not this time.

"What you fail to understand is that I don't want to be *engaged* to you, either." She held up a hand to stop him from talking, and the sheet slipped again, just enough to afford him a glimpse of one, rose-hued nipple.

His body went hard again. Perfect. Just perfect.

Diana glanced down at him, then back up. There wasn't a trace of desire in her eyes this time. "I can't talk to you about this while you're naked. Get dressed and meet me in the kitchen."

She flounced away, leaving Franco alone in a room that throbbed with memories.

He shoved his legs into his tuxedo pants from the night before and splashed some water on his face in the bathroom. When he strode into the kitchen, he found her standing at the coffeemaker, still dressed in the bedsheet. Lulu was frolicking at her feet, engaged in a fierce game of tug-of-war with a corner of the sheet. The dog didn't even register his presence. Clearly, the two of them had bonded, just as he'd hoped. He should have been happy. Instead, he felt distinctly outnumbered.

Diana poured a steaming cup, and Franco looked at it longingly.

She glanced at him, but didn't offer him any.

Not that he'd expected it.

"I'm sorry," he said quietly.

She lifted a brow. "For what, exactly?"

For everything.

He sighed. "I should have given you a heads-up."

Her expression softened ever so slightly. "You tried."

"I could have tried harder." He took a step closer and caught a glimpse of his reflection—moody and blue—in the sapphire still hanging around her neck.

She backed up against the counter, maintaining the space between them. "Just tell me why. I need to know."

A muscle flexed in Franco's jaw. This wasn't a conversation he wanted to have the morning after they'd slept together. Or ever, to be honest. "My chances of getting back on the Kingsmen will be much greater if I'm engaged."

She blinked. "That doesn't make sense."

Don't make me explain it. He gave her a look of warning. "It matters. Trust me."

"Trust you?" She set her coffee cup on the counter and crossed her arms. "You've got to be kidding."

"For the record, it would be even better if we were married." What was he saying? He was willing to go pretty far to get his job back, but not that far.

Diana gaped at him. "I can't believe this. You're a polo player, not a priest. What does your marital status have to do with anything…" Her eyes grew narrow. "Unless… oh, my God…"

Franco held up his hands. "I can explain."

But he couldn't. Not in any kind of way that Diana would find acceptable. Even if he broke his promise to

Luc and told her the truth, she'd never believe him. Not in this lifetime.

"You did something bad, didn't you? Some kind of terrible sexual misconduct." She fiddled with the stone around her neck, and Franco couldn't help but notice the way her fingers trembled. He hated himself a little bit right then. "Go ahead and tell me. What was it? Did you sleep with someone's wife this time?"

He looked at her long and hard.

"You did," she said flatly. The final sparks of whatever magic had happened between them the night before vanished from her gaze. All Franco could see in the depths of her violet eyes was hurt. And thinly veiled hatred. "How could I be such an idiot? *Again?* Who was it?"

Less than an hour ago, she'd been asleep with her head on his chest as their hearts beat in unison. How had everything turned so spectacularly to crap since then?

A grim numbness blossomed in Franco's chest. He knew exactly what had gone wrong. The past had found its way into their present.

Didn't it always?

He'd written the script of this conversation years ago.

He wanted to sweep her hair from her face and force her to look him in the eye so she could see the real him. He wanted to take her back to bed and whisper things he'd never told anyone else as he pushed his way inside her again.

He wanted to tell her the truth.

"It was Natalie Ellis," he said quietly.

"Ellis? As in *Jack* Ellis?" She pulled the bedsheet tighter around her curves, much to Franco's dismay. "You had an affair with your boss's wife? That's despicable, Franco. Even for you. You must think I'm the biggest fool you've ever met."

"I'm the fool," he said.

She shook her head. "Don't, okay? Just don't be nice to me right now. Please."

"Diana…"

Before he could say another word, the cell phone in the pocket of his tuxedo pants chimed with an incoming text message.

Damn it.

Diana rolled her eyes. Lulu barked at the phone in solidarity. "Go ahead. Look at it. It's probably from one of your married girlfriends. Don't let me stand in your way."

Franco didn't make a move. Whoever was texting him could wait.

His phone chimed again.

Diana glared at him. "You disgust me, Franco. And I swear, if you don't answer that right now, I'm going to reach into your pocket and do it for you."

Franco sighed and looked at the phone's display.

See you at practice today at 10 sharp. Come ready to play. Don't be late.

The engagement announcement had worked. He was back on the team.

And back on Diana's bad side.

She hated him.

Again.

Chapter Fourteen

Diana didn't bother returning Artem's call. Instead, she decided to get dressed and go straight to Drake Diamonds and explain things in person.

But there was no actual explanation, was there? She was engaged. *Pretend* engaged, but still. Engaged.

She had no idea what she was going to say to her brother. If she admitted she'd known nothing about the engagement, it would look like she'd lost control over her own public image. And as VP of public relations, the Drake image was pretty much the one thing she was responsible for. On the other hand, if she pretended she'd known all about the faux engagement, Artem would be furious that she'd kept him in the dark. It was a catch-22. Either way, she was screwed.

She had to face him sooner or later, though. She desperately wanted to get it over with. Maybe she'd go ahead and tell him he'd been right. The charade had gone too far. She should end it. The Lambertis would walk away, of course. And she'd never be co-CEO. She might not even be able to keep her current position. Artem had told her she'd proven herself, but that had been before the engagement fiasco. Who knew what would happen if she broke up with her fake boyfriend now? She could end up right back in the Engagements department.

But that would be better than having to walk around pretending she was going to get married to Franco, wouldn't it?

Yes.

No.

Maybe.

The only thing she knew for certain was that she shouldn't have slept with him the night before. How could she have been so monumentally stupid? She deserved to be fired. She'd fire herself if she could.

He'd carried on an affair with a married woman. That was a new low, even for a playboy like Franco. And it made him no different than her father.

So, of course she'd jumped into bed with him. God, she hated herself.

"Is he in?" she asked Mrs. Barnes, glancing nervously at the closed office door. What was her brother doing in there? He rarely kept his door closed. He was probably throwing darts at the wedding page of the *Times*. Or possibly interviewing new candidates for the VP of public relations position. She shook her head. "Never mind, I know he wants to see me. I'm going in."

"Wait!" Mrs. Barnes called after her.

It was too late, though. Diana had already flung Artem's door open and stormed inside. Artem sat behind his desk, just as she'd expected. But he wasn't alone. Carla and Don Lamberti occupied the two chairs opposite him.

Ophelia was also there, standing beside the desk with what looked like a crystal baseball.

The diamond.

It was even larger than Diana had imagined. She paused just long enough to take in its impressive size and to notice the way it reflected light, even in its uncut state. It practically glowed in Ophelia's hands.

All four heads in the office turned in her direction.

Any and all hopes she had of sneaking out the door unnoticed were officially dashed. "I'm so sorry. I didn't mean to interrupt."

She practically ran out of the office, but of course she wasn't fast enough.

"Diana, what a nice surprise!" The brightness of Carla Lamberti's smile rivaled that of her diamond.

Diana forced a smile and cursed the four-inch Jimmy Choos that had prevented her speedy getaway. Why, oh why, had she worn stilettos?

Probably because there had been a dozen paparazzi following her every move all day, thanks to Franco's little engagement announcement. The doorman had warned her about the crowd of photographers gathered outside her building before she'd left the apartment. If her picture was going to be splashed on the front page of every newspaper in town, she was going to look decent. Especially considering that Franco's walk of shame out of her building earlier in the morning had already turned up on no less than four websites.

Not only had she made the terrible mistake of sleeping with him, but now everyone with a Wi-Fi connection knew all about it.

"It looks like you're busy. I just needed to talk to Artem, but it can wait." She turned and headed for the door.

"Don't be silly. Join us. We insist. Right, Mr. Drake?" Carla glanced questioningly at Artem, who nodded his agreement. "I want to hear all about your engagement to Mr. Andrade. I can't seem to pry a word out of your brother."

The older woman turned to face Diana again. Behind her back, Artem crooked a finger at Diana, then pointed to the empty place on his office sofa.

Okay, then. Diana took a deep breath, crossed the room and sat down.

"So, tell us everything. As I said, Artem won't breathe a word about your wedding." Carla cast a mock look of reprimand in Artem's direction.

Your wedding.

Diana did her best not to vomit right there on the Drake-blue carpet.

Ever the diplomat, Ophelia jumped into the conversation. "I'm sure Diana and Franco would like to keep some things private. It's more special that way, don't you think?"

Diana released a breath she hadn't realized she'd been holding. She owed Ophelia. Big-time.

Mr. Lamberti rested a hand on his wife's knee. "Goodness, dear. Leave Diana alone. She's here to join our meeting about the plans for the diamond, not to discuss the intimate details of her personal life."

Carla let out a laugh and shrugged. "I suppose that's true. Please pardon my manners. I was just so excited to read about your engagement in the paper this morning. I knew from the moment I saw you and Franco together at the Harry Winston party that you were destined to be together. The way that man looks at you…"

Her voice drifted off, and she sighed dreamily.

Artem cleared his throat. "Shall we proceed with the

meeting? Ophelia has drawn up some beautiful designs for the stone."

"Of course. Just one more question. I promise it's the last one." Mrs. Lamberti's gaze shifted once again to Diana. She prayed for the sofa to somehow open itself up and swallow her whole, but of course it didn't. "It's true, isn't it? Are you and Mr. Andrade really engaged to be married?"

This was the opening she'd been waiting for. She could end the nonsensical charade right here and now, and she'd never even have to set eyes on Franco again. All she had to do was say no. The papers had made a mistake. She and Franco weren't engaged. In fact, they were no longer seeing each other. The Lambertis would obviously be disappointed, but surely they wouldn't pack up their diamond and leave.

Would they?

Diana swallowed. *Do it. Just do it.*

Why was she hesitating? This was her chance to get her life back. It was now or never. If she didn't fess up, she'd be stuck indefinitely as Franco's fiancée.

Speak now or forever hold your peace.

She was already thinking in terms of wedding language. Perfect. She may as well climb right into a Vera Wang.

She glanced from the Lambertis to Artem to Ophelia. This would have been so much easier without an audience. And without that ridiculously huge diamond staring her in the face. It was blinding. Which was the only rational explanation for the next words that came out of her mouth.

"Of course it's true." She smiled her most radiant, bridal grin. "We're absolutely engaged."

* * *

All the way to Bridgehampton, Franco waited for the other shoe to drop. He fully expected to arrive at practice only to be ousted again. The moment he'd left Diana's apartment, she'd no doubt picked up the phone and called every newspaper in town to demand a retraction.

He wasn't sure what to make of the fact that she hadn't. His cell phone sat on the passenger seat of his Jag, conspicuously silent.

He arrived at the Kingsmen practice field at ten sharp just as instructed, despite having to break a few traffic laws to get there on time. He still hadn't heard a word from Diana when he climbed out of his car and tossed his cell into the duffel bag that carried his gear.

He needed to quit worrying about her. About the two of them. Especially since they weren't an actual couple.

It had only been hate sex.

He slammed the door of his Jag hard enough to make the car shake.

"And here I thought you'd be thrilled to be back," someone said.

Franco turned to find Coach Santos standing behind him. "Good morning."

"Is it? Because you seem pissed as hell." His gaze swept Franco from top to bottom. "A tuxedo? At ten in the morning? This doesn't bode well, son."

Franco was lucky he kept a bag packed with his practice gear in the trunk of his car. There hadn't been time to stop by his apartment. "Relax. I wasn't out partying. You caught me at my fiancée's apartment this morning. I'm a changed man, remember?"

"Let's hope so. Ellis isn't so sure, but he's willing to give it a shot. For now." Santos looked pointedly at Franco's rumpled tux shirt. "But try not to arrive at practice look-

ing like you just rolled out of someone's bed. It's not helping your cause. Got it?"

"Got it." Franco gave him a curt nod and tried not to
think about that bed. Or that particular *someone*.

He needed to have his head in the game, today more
than ever. But he hated the way he and Diana had left
things. He'd thought this time would be different.

If he was being honest with himself though, it was for
the best. Diana Drake had always been out of his league.
He didn't have a thing to offer her.

Time hadn't changed who he was. It hadn't changed
anything. He and Diana had ended back where they'd
begun.

"We've got a scrimmage in an hour. And don't forget
about Argentine Night at the Polo Club tonight. Ellis ex-
pects you there with your doting fiancée on your arm."

Franco's gut churned. Getting Diana anywhere near
the Polo Club would be next to impossible. It seemed as
though she hadn't gotten within a mile radius of a live
horse since her accident.

There was also the slight complication that she hated
him. Now, more than ever.

"What are you waiting for? Get suited up." Coach
Santos jerked his head in the direction of the practice
field, where the grooms were already getting the horses
saddled up and ready.

Before Franco had come to America—before all the
championship trophies and the late-night after parties—
he'd been a groom. He'd been the one who brushed the
horses, running a curry comb over them until the Argentine sunshine reflected off them like a mirror. He'd
bathed them in the evenings, grinning as they tossed
their heads and whinnied beneath the spray of the water
hose. Franco had lived and breathed horses back then.

When he wasn't shoveling out stalls, he was on horse-back, practicing his swing, learning the game of polo.

Sometimes he missed those days.

But grooms didn't become champions, at least not where Franco had come from. He was one of the lucky ones. Not lucky, actually. Chosen. He owed Luc Piero everything.

"You did it, man." Luc greeted Franco with a bone-crushing hug the moment he stepped onto the field. "You're back."

"I told you there wasn't anything to worry about." Franco shrugged and fastened his helmet in place.

"Engaged, though?" Luc lifted a brow. "Tell me that's not real."

"Does it matter?" Franco planted one of his feet into a stirrup, grabbed onto the saddle and swung himself onto his horse's back. His grooms had gotten the horses to the field just in the nick of time.

"Yes, it matters. It matters a whole hell of a lot. I mean, you've never been the marrying kind."

"So I hear." He was being an ass, and he knew it. But he wasn't in the mood to discuss his marriageability. Not when he couldn't shake the memory of the hurt in Diana's gaze this morning.

He sighed. "Sorry. I just don't want to discuss Diana Drake. Or any of the Drakes, for that matter."

They had been the means to an end. Nothing more. Why did he keep having to remind himself of that fact?

Luc shrugged. "I can live with that. You're back. That's what important. Nothing else. Right?"

Franco shot him a grim smile. "Absolutely."

He rode hard once the scrimmage got underway. Fast. Aggressive.

By the close of the fourth chukker, the halfway point

of the game, the scoreboard read 11 to 0. Franco had scored each and every one of the goals. He managed four more before the end of the game. He was back, indeed.

His teammates gathered round to congratulate him. Ellis applauded from his box seat, but didn't approach Franco. And that was fine. Franco didn't feel much like talking. To Ellis or anyone. The urge he felt to check his cell phone for messages was every bit as frustrating as it was pressing. When he finally did, he had over forty voicemails, all from various members of the media.

Not a single word from Diana.

He shoved his phone in his back pocket and slammed his locker closed. What was he supposed to do now? Were he and Diana engaged? Were they over?

He had no idea.

He stopped by his apartment in Tribeca and packed a bag, just in case. No news was good news. Wasn't that the old adage? Besides, he couldn't quite shake the feeling that if Diana Drake had decided to dump him, he would have heard it first from the press…

Because that's how monumentally screwed up their fake relationship was.

But the mob of photographers outside Diana's building didn't say a word about a breakup when Franco arrived on the scene. They screamed the usual questions at him, along with a few new ones. About the wedding, of course. He kept his head down and did his best to ignore them.

The doorman waved Franco upstairs, just as he had before. That didn't necessarily mean anything. Diana probably wouldn't have broken the news first to her doorman, but Franco was beginning to feel more confident that he, indeed, had a fiancée waiting for him in the penthouse.

Sure enough, when Diana answered the door, there

was a colossal diamond solitaire situated on her ring finger. "Oh, it's you."

For some nonsensical reason, the sight of the ring rubbed Franco the wrong way. If their engagement had been real, he would have chosen a diamond himself. And it wouldn't be a generic rock like the one on her hand. He would have selected something special. Unique.

But what the hell was he thinking? *None* of this was real. The ring shouldn't matter.

It did, though. He had no idea why, but it mattered.

"Nice ring," he said through gritted teeth.

"I picked it up at Drake Diamonds today since my *fiancé* forgot to give me one." She lifted an accusatory brow. "What are you doing here, anyway?"

He gave her a grim smile and swished past her with his duffle and a garment bag slung over his shoulder. "Honey, I'm home."

She gaped at him. "I beg your pardon?"

Lulu shot toward him, all happy barks and wagging tail. At least someone was happy to see him. He tossed his bags on the sofa and gathered the puppy into his arms.

Diana frowned at Lulu, then back at Franco. *Someone looks jealous.* "What's going on? Surely you don't think you're moving in with me."

"We're engaged, remember? This is what engaged people do."

She shook her head. "Please tell me you're not serious. I've already taken in one stray. Isn't that enough?"

It was the wrong thing to say.

"You're comparing me to a stray dog now?" he said through clenched teeth.

She opened her mouth to say something, but Franco wouldn't let her. He'd heard enough.

"I've put up with a hell of a lot from you and your family in the past few weeks, Diana. But you will not speak to me that way. Is that understood, wifey?"

She blinked. "I..."

He held up a hand. "Save it. We can talk later. We have a date tonight, anyway. You should get dressed."

"A *date*?"

"We're going to Argentine Night at the Polo Club. If you have a problem with it, I don't want to hear it. I've accompanied you to every gala and party under the sun in the past few weeks. You can do one thing for me." He gave Lulu a scratch behind the ears. "Unless you'd like to kick both of the strays out of your life once and for all?"

She wouldn't dare. If she wanted him gone, she wouldn't be wearing that sparkling diamond on her ring finger. Franco honestly didn't know why she wanted to play along with the engagement, but he no longer cared.

You care. You know you do.

If he didn't, the stray dog comment wouldn't have gotten under his skin the way it had.

"Well?" he asked.

"I'll be ready in half an hour." She plucked the dog from his arms. "And Lulu isn't going anywhere."

She sauntered past him with the little pug's face peering at him over her shoulder and slammed the bedroom door.

Franco wanted to stay angry. Anger was good. Anger was comfortable. He knew a lot more about what to do with anger than about what to do with the feelings that had swirled between them last night.

But seeing her with the dog took the edge off. He'd been right to force the puppy on her. He'd done something good.

For once in his life.

Chapter Fifteen

Diana had spent the better part of her life around horses, but she'd never been to the Polo Club in Bridgehampton. Show jumping and polo were clearly two separate sports. She'd known polo players before, obviously. She'd certainly seen Franco at her fair share of equestrian events. But she'd never run in the same after-hours circles as Franco's crowd.

Even before the night she'd lost her virginity to Franco, she'd noticed a brooding intensity about those athletes that both fascinated and frightened her. They rode hard and they play hard. Deep down, she knew that was one of the qualities about Franco that had first drawn her toward him. He didn't care what anyone else had to say about him. He behaved any way he chose. Both on and off the field.

Diana had no idea what that might feel like. She was a Drake, and that name came with a myriad of expectations.

If she'd been born a boy, things would have been different. Drake men were immune to rules and expectations. At least, that had been the case with her father. He'd spent money as he wished and slept with whomever he wished, and everyone in the family had to just deal with it. Her mother included.

"You look awfully serious all of a sudden," Franco said as she stepped out of the Drake limousine at the valet stand outside the Polo Club. "What are you thinking about?"

"Nothing." *Marriage.* Why was she even pondering such things? Oh, yeah, because she was engaged now. "I'm fine. Let's just go inside."

"Very well." He lifted her hand and kissed it before tucking it into the crook of his elbow.

Diana looked around, expecting to see a group of photographers clustered by the entrance of the club. But she didn't spot a single telephoto lens.

"Good evening, Mr. Andrade and Miss Drake." A valet held the door open for them as Franco led her into the foyer.

"Wow," she whispered. "This is really something."

The stately white building had been transformed into a South American wonderland of twinkling lights and rich, red decor. Sultry tango music filled the air. Diana was suddenly very glad she'd chosen a red lace gown for the occasion.

She and Franco were situated at a round table near the center of the room, along with his coach and several other players and their wives. When she took her seat, the man beside her introduced himself as Luc Piero.

"It's a pleasure to meet you," she said.

"The pleasure's all mine, I assure you." Luc grinned from ear to ear. "I've known Franco for a long time, and

I've never seen him as captivated with anyone before as he is with you. I've told him time and again that I wanted to meet you, but he's been hiding you away."

"I've done no such thing," Franco countered.

"That's right. Your pictures have been in the newspaper every day for two weeks running. How could I forget?" Luc smiled.

Diana kind of liked him. She probably would have liked him more if she weren't so busy searching the room for Natalie Ellis. She had a morbid curiosity about the woman Franco had apparently considered worth risking his entire career over. Diana had seen the woman on a handful of occasions, but she wanted a better look. She wasn't jealous, obviously. Simply curious.

Right. You're a card-carrying green-eyed monster right now.

"I'm going to go get us some drinks, darling." Franco bent to kiss her on the cheek, which pleased her far more than it should have. "I'll be right back."

She reminded herself for the millionth time that she hated him, then turned to Luc. "You say you've known Franco a long time?"

"All our lives. We grew up together in Argentina."

"Really?" Franco had never breathed a word to her about his childhood. She couldn't help being curious about the way he'd grown up. "Tell me more."

"He's loved horses since before he could walk. You know that, right?"

She didn't. But she understood it all too well. "That's something we have in common."

"My father owned one of the local polo clubs in Buenos Aires. I used to hang out there when I was a kid, and that's where I met Franco."

"Oh, was he taking riding lessons there?"

Luc gave her an odd glance. "No, Franco's one hundred percent self-taught. A natural. He was a groom at my father's stable."

"I see." She nodded as if this wasn't stunning new information. After all, she should probably have some sort of clue about Franco's childhood since he was her fiancé.

But a groom?

In the equestrian world, grooms and riders belonged in two very different social classes. Not that Diana liked or condoned dividing people into such groups. But it was an unpleasant fact of life—she'd never known a groom who had gone on to compete in show jumping. Maybe things were different in the sport of polo.

Then again, maybe not.

"It's unusual, I know. But Franco was different, right from the start."

Indeed. Her throat grew tight.

She should be furious with him after the stunt he'd pulled. He'd strong-armed her into an engagement, plain and simple. An engagement she didn't want.

And she'd let him. She wasn't sure who she was angrier at—Franco or herself.

"Different. How so?" She glanced at Franco across the room, where he stood standing beside a man she recognized from equestrian circles as Jack Ellis, the owner of the Kingsmen.

Her breath caught in her throat. No matter how many times she looked at Franco—whether it was from the other side of a crowded room or beside him in bed—his physical perfection always seemed to catch her off guard. He was the most handsome man she'd ever seen. Ellis, on the other hand, appeared immune to Franco's charms. The expression on his face was grim. Even the woman on Jack Ellis's arm didn't seem to notice Franco's charming smile or dark, chiseled beauty. Natalie Ellis looked almost bored as she glanced around the room. When her gaze fell on Luc, her lips curved into a nearly imperceptible smile.

Odd.

"Well…" Luc continued, dragging her attention back to their conversation. "Like I said, he was a talented rider. Fearless. Instinctual. Even as a kid, I knew I was witnessing something special. He had a bond with the horses like nothing I'd ever seen. They were his life."

A chill went up Diana's spine. She had a feeling she was about to hear something she shouldn't.

"His life," she echoed.

"I found out he was sleeping in the stables and kept it a secret from my father for over year before he found out." Luc gave her a sad smile. "I thought he'd be angry and kick Franco out. Instead, he gave Franco a room in our family home."

She most definitely shouldn't be hearing this. Franco had never said a thing to her about his life in Argentina. Now she knew why. These were the sort of intimate details only a lover should know. A real lover.

She should change the subject. Delving further into this conversation would be an invasion of Franco's privacy. But she was so distraught by what she'd heard that she couldn't string together a single coherent sentence.

She'd called Franco a stray.

And he'd been homeless.

Oh, God.

"Are you all right, Diana?" Luc was watching her with guarded curiosity. "You look like you've seen a ghost."

No, just a monster. And that monster is me.

"Fine." She cleared her throat. "Is that when Franco

started playing polo? After he moved in with your family?"

Luc shrugged. "Yes and no. He was still working as a groom, but I'd begun playing. Franco was my training partner. In the beginning, he was just there to help me improve my game. That didn't last long."

"He's that good, isn't he?" She forced herself to smile like a doting bride.

What was happening? She was acting just like the nauseatingly sweet engaged couples she'd loathed so much when she worked in Engagements.

It *was* an act, wasn't it?

"He's the best. He always has been. His talent transcends any traditional rules of the game. That's why my father put him on the team." He smiled at Franco as he approached the table. "We've been teammates ever since."

A lump formed in Diana's throat. "I'm glad. Franco deserves a friend like you."

"He's more like a brother than a friend. He's always got my back. The guy's loyal to a fault, but I'm sure you know that by now."

Loyal to a fault…

Before Franco had walked through the door of Drake Diamonds a month ago, Diana would have never used those to words to describe him. Now she wasn't so sure.

She'd seen a different side to Franco in recent weeks. It all made sense now…the way he'd jumped at the chance to adopt a homeless puppy, his commitment to their fake relationship. Franco was a man of his word.

She was beginning to question everything she'd believed about him, and that wasn't good. It wasn't good at all. Their entire relationship had been built on a lie, and Diana preferred it that way. At least she knew where she stood. She operated best when she could look at the world in black and white. But things with Franco had blurred into a disturbing shade of gray.

She didn't know what she thought anymore. Worse, she wasn't sure what she felt. Because despite everything that had happened in the past, and despite the fact that just when she thought she could trust Franco he'd gone and announced to the world that they were engaged, she felt something for him. And that *something* scared the life out of her.

But he obviously had little or no regard for marriage, otherwise he wouldn't have bedded Natalie Ellis. Natalie Ellis, who seemed to have no interest in Franco whatsoever.

What was going on?

"Hello, darling. Sorry to leave you alone for so long." Franco bent and kissed her on the cheek again. "I hope Luc hasn't been boring you."

"No, not at all." Quite the opposite, actually.

She smiled up at him and tried to forget all the things she'd just heard. But it was no use. She couldn't shake the image of Franco as a young boy, sleeping on a bed of straw in a barn. What had happened to him to make him end up there? Where was his family? So many unanswered questions.

The air between them was heavy with secrets and lies, but somewhere deep inside Diana, an unsettling truth had begun to blossom.

She had feelings for Franco. Genuine feelings.

"The tango contest is about to begin." He offered her his hand. "Dance with me?"

She stared at his outstretched palm, and words began to spin in her head.

Do you take this man to love and to cherish, all the days of your life?

She was losing it.

"Yes." *I do.* She placed her hand in his. She didn't even know how to tango, but she didn't much care at this point. "Yes, please."

The music started and Franco wrapped his right arm around Diana until his hand rested squarely in the center of her back. When he lifted his left arm, she placed her hand gently in his.

"I should probably mention that I don't exactly know how to tango." She blushed.

"Not to worry. I'm a rather strong lead."

"Why am I not surprised?" she murmured. He took a step forward, and she moved with him in perfect synchrony. "Luc had some lovely things to say about you just now."

They reached the end of the club's small dance floor, and Franco spun her around. "He's probably had more than his fair share of champagne."

"Don't." Diana shook her head and slid one of her stilettos up the length of his leg. "I'm being serious. He loves you like a brother."

Franco nodded. Her leg had traveled nearly up to his hip. He pulled her incrementally closer. "You're right. He does. And I'd do anything for him."

He deliberately avoided glancing in Natalie Ellis's direction.

This wasn't the time or place for a heart-to-heart, but something about the way Diana was looking at him all of a sudden made it impossible for him to keep giving her flippant responses.

She slid her foot back to the floor and they resumed stalking each other across the floor to the strains of the accordion music.

"I had no idea you could dance like this, Franco."
Diana swiveled in his arms. "You're full of surprises."

"It's an Argentine dance." He lifted her in the air, and
her legs wrapped around his waist, then flared out before she landed on the floor with a whisper. For someone who claimed not to know how to tango, Diana was
holding her own. Someone had clearly been watching
Dancing With the Stars.

This was beginning to feel less like dancing and more
like sex. Not that Franco was complaining.

"Tell me more about your life in Argentina," she whispered as her hand crept to the back of his neck.

Should he be this aroused at a social function? Definitely not. He was a grown man not a horny fifteen-year-
old kid. "Other than the dancing?"

"Yes, although I'm a little curious about the dancing, as well."

He pulled her closer, but kept his gaze glued in the
opposite direction. The quintessential tango posture.
Convenient, as well, since he never discussed his family upbringing. But he'd witnessed a staggering amount
of Drake family dynamics over the past few weeks. Hell,
he was beginning to almost feel like a Drake himself. If
she was asking questions, he owed her a certain degree
of transparency.

"I grew up with a single mother in Barrio de la Boca.
I never knew my father."

"I see," she murmured.

He cast a sideways glance in her direction, hoping
against hope he wouldn't see a trace of pity in her gaze.
Having Diana Drake look at him in such a way would
have killed him. She wasn't, though. She seemed more
curious than anything, and for that, Franco was grateful.

"My mother was less than attentive. I ran away when

I was eleven. Luc's father took me in. The rest is history, as they say."

They reached the end of the dance floor again, but instead of turning around, Diana slid her foot up the back of his calf. "I wish I would have known about this sooner."

He reached for the back of her thigh and ground subtly against her before letting her let go. "Would it have changed anything?"

"Yes." She swallowed, and he traced the movement up and down the elegant column of her neck. "I'm sorry, Franco. I should have never said what I did earlier."

He lowered her into a deep dip and echoed her own words back to her from the night before. "You're forgiven."

"Ladies and gentlemen, the winners of the annual tango contest are Franco Andrade and Diana Drake."

The room burst into applause.

"I can't believe this," Diana said as Franco pulled her upright. "We won!"

Franco wove his hand through hers and held on tightly as Jack Ellis approached them, holding a shiny silver trophy.

His mouth curved into a tight smile as he offered it to Franco. "Congratulations."

"Gracias." The fact that Ellis was so clearly upset by his presence probably should have bothered Franco to some extent, but he couldn't bring himself to care at the moment.

Diana was speaking to him again. They'd only exchanged a handful of words since their engagement had been announced, and somehow he'd managed to get back in her good graces. Better than that, it felt genuine. He was starting to feel close to her in a way he seldom did with anyone.

Don't fool yourself. It's only temporary, remember.

"Miss Drake, it's a pleasure to make your acquaintance." Ellis shook Diana's hand. "Will you be joining us at tomorrow's match?"

Diana went instantly pale. "Tomorrow's match?"

"The Kingsmen have a game tomorrow. Surely Franco's mentioned it." Ellis frowned.

A spike of irritation hit Franco hard in his chest. Ellis could talk to him however he liked, but he wasn't about to let his boss be anything but polite to Diana. "Of course I have. Unfortunately, Diana has a previous engagement."

She nodded. After an awkward, silent beat, she followed his lead. "I'm afraid Franco's right. I have a commitment tomorrow that I simply can't get out of."

"That's too bad," Ellis said. "Another time, perhaps."

"Perhaps." She smiled, but Franco could see the panic in her amethyst gaze. She had no intention of watching him on horseback. Not tomorrow. Not ever.

Ellis said his goodbyes and walked away. The band began to play again, and Franco and Diana were swallowed up by other couples.

"Come with me." He slid his arm around her and whispered into her hair.

"Where are we going?" She peered up at him, and he could still see a trace of fear in those luminous eyes.

Franco would have given everything he had to take her distress away. But no amount of money or success could replace what she'd lost the day she'd fallen. He'd never felt so helpless in his life. Nothing he could do would bring Diamond back to life.

But maybe, just maybe, he could help her remember what it had been like to be fearless.

If only she would let him.

* * *

"Close your eyes," Franco whispered. His breath was hot on her neck in tantalizing contrast to the cool night air on her face.

Franco's voice was deep, insistent. Despite the warning bells going off in Diana's head, she did as he asked.

"Good girl."

A thrill coursed through her and settled low in her belly. What was she doing? She shouldn't be out here in the dark, taking orders from this man. She most definitely shouldn't be turned on by it.

She inhaled a shaky breath. *Open your eyes. Just open your eyes and walk away.*

But she knew she wouldn't. Couldn't if she tried. Something had happened out there on the dance floor. She felt as if she'd seen Franco for the first time. She'd gotten a glimpse of his past, and somehow that made the dance more meaningful. Not just their tango…the three-year dance they'd been engaged in since they'd first met.

"This way." His hand settled onto the small of her back. "Keep your eyes shut."

He started walking. Slowly. Diana kept in step beside him, letting him lead her. Unable to see, her other senses went on high alert. The sweet smell of hay and horses tickled her nose. The light touch of Franco's fingertips felt decadent, more intimate than it should have.

She licked her lips and let herself remember what it had felt like to take those fingertips into her mouth, to suck gently on them while he'd watched through eyes glittering like black diamonds. She wanted to feel that way again. She wanted *him* again, God help her.

"Be careful." Franco's footsteps slowed. She heard a door sliding open.

"Can I open my eyes now?" He voice was breathy, barely more than a whisper.

Franco's hand slid lower, perilously close to her bottom. "No, you may not."

How close was his face? Close enough to kiss? Close enough for her to lean toward him and take his bottom lip gently between her teeth?

She swallowed. This shouldn't be happening. None of it. The sad reality of Franco's childhood shouldn't change the ridiculous truth of their situation. The only thing they shared was a long string of lies. This was the same man who'd called the newspapers and told them he was marrying her. It was the same man who'd so callously dismissed her the morning after she'd lost her virginity.

They were pretending.

But it no longer felt that way. Not now that she'd seen the real him.

"Franco," she whispered, reaching for him.

He caught her wrist midair. "Shhhh. Let me."

She waited for a beat and wondered what would come next. Franco slid her hand into his, intertwining their fingers. Then her hand made contact with something soft. Warm. Alive.

She stiffened.

"It's okay, Diana. Keep your eyes closed. I'm here. I've got you." Franco's other arm wrapped around her, pulling her against him. He stood behind her with his hand still covering hers, moving it in slow circles over velvety softness.

A horse. She was touching a horse. She knew without opening her eyes.

I'm here. I've got you.

Did he know this was the closest she'd come to a horse since she'd fallen? Did he know this was the first time she'd touched one since that awful day? Could he possibly?

Of course he did. Because he saw her. He always had.

She felt a tear slide down her cheek, and she squeezed her eyes shut even harder. If she opened them now and saw her fingers interlocked with Franco's, moving slowly over the magnificent animal in front of them, she wouldn't be able to take it. She'd fall apart. She'd fall...

But this time, Franco would be there to catch her.

Or not.

How could this man be the same one who'd slept with Natalie Ellis and gotten himself fired?

It didn't make sense. Especially now that she knew his background. She could see why he pushed people away. She could even see why he'd said such awful things after she'd slept with him three years ago. Intimacy—real intimacy—didn't come easily to Franco. It couldn't. Not after what he'd been through as a boy.

If anyone could understand that, Diana could. Hadn't her own childhood been filled with a similar brand of confusion? They'd each found their escape on horseback. Which is why nothing about his termination made sense.

Polo meant everything to Franco. More than she'd ever imagined. Why would he risk it for a meaningless romp with his boss's wife?

There had to be more to the story. She wished he would tell her, but she knew deep down he never would. And she didn't particularly blame him.

"I lied, Franco." She kept her eyes closed. She couldn't quite bring herself to look at him. "It wasn't hate sex."

"I know it wasn't." He pulled her closer against him. When he spoke, his lips brushed lightly against the curve of her neck, leaving a trail of goose bumps in their wake.

"I don't hate you. I never did." She was crying in earnest now. Tears were streaming down her face, but she didn't care. She was tired of the lies. So very tired.

"Don't cry, Wildfire. Please don't cry." He pressed an openmouthed kiss to her shoulder. "It kills me to see you hurting. It always did, even back then."

Her heart pounded hard in her chest. There were more things to say, more lies to correct. She wanted to set the record straight. She *needed* to. Even if she never saw him again after next week.

You won't. He's going away, and he's not coming back.

"For three years, I've been telling myself I chose you because I knew you'd let me down. It's not true. I chose you because I wanted you. I wanted you back then. I wanted you the other night. And I want you now." She opened her eyes and turned to face him.

They were standing in a barn. She'd known as much, and she'd expected to feel panicked when confronted with the sight of the horses in their stalls. But she didn't. She felt right, somehow. Safe.

She'd dreaded coming here tonight, and now she realized it had been a gift.

"How did you know this is what I needed?" she asked.

He cupped her face, tipped her chin upward so she looked him in the eyes. "I knew because, in many ways, you and I are the same. I want you, too, Diana. I want you so much I can barely see straight."

"Take me home, Franco."

Chapter Sixteen

Franco didn't dare touch Diana in the backseat of the limo on their ride back to New York. If he did, he wouldn't be able to stop himself from making love to her right there in plain view of the driver and every other car on the long stretch of highway between Bridgehampton and the city.

It was more than just an exercise in restraint. It was the longest ninety minutes of his life.

They rode side by side, each trying not to look at the other for fear they'd lose control. An electric current passed between them. If the spark had been visible, it would have filled the lux interior of the car with diamond light.

As the dizzying lights of Manhattan came into view, he allowed his gaze to roam. It wandered down Diana's elegant throat, lingering on the tantalizing dip between her collarbones—the place where he most wanted to kiss her at the moment so he could feel the wild beating of her pulse beneath his lips. He wanted to taste the decadent passion she had for life. Consume it.

Diana felt each and every one of her emotions to its fullest extent. It was one of the things he'd always loved about her. Being by her side these past weeks had caused Franco to realize the extent to which he avoided feelings. Since he'd moved to America, he'd done his level best to forget the world he'd left behind. His memories of Argentina were laden with shame. The shame of growing up without a father. The shame of the way his mother had all but abandoned him.

He'd tried to outrun that shame on the polo field. He'd tried to drown it in women and wine. But it had always been there, simmering beneath the surface, preventing him from forming any real sort of connection with anyone. At times he even kept Luc at arm's length.

Luc knew the rules. He knew not to bring up the past. He knew not to push. Why he may have done so this evening was a mystery Franco didn't care to examine too closely.

He thinks this is different. He thinks you're in love.

This *was* different.

Was it love? Franco didn't know. Didn't want to know. Because what he and Diana had together came with an expiration date. He'd known as much from the start, but for some reason it was just beginning to sink in. The date was growing closer. Just a matter of days away. And now that he was a member of the Kingsmen again, he'd be leaving just as soon as their arrangement came to an end.

He should be happy. Elated, even. This was why he'd gotten himself tangled up with the Drakes to begin with. This was what he'd wanted.

But as his gaze traveled lower, past the midnight blue

stone that glittered against Diana's porcelain skin, he had the crippling sensation that everything he wanted was right beside him. Within arm's reach.

Screw the waiting.

He pushed the button that raised the limo's privacy divider and slid toward her across the wide gulf of leather seat in under a second. Diana let out a tiny gasp as his mouth crushed down on hers, hot and needy. But then her hands were sliding inside his tuxedo jacket, pulling him closer. And closer, until he could feel the fierce beat of her heart against his chest.

Not here. Take it slow.

But he couldn't stop his hands from reaching for the zipper at her back and lowering it until the bodice of her dress fell away, exposing the decadent perfection of her breasts. He stared, transfixed, as he dragged the pad of his thumb across one of her nipples with a featherlight touch.

The gemstone nestled in her cleavage seemed to glow like liquid fire, burning blue. On some level, Franco knew this wasn't possible. But he'd lost the ability for rational thought. All he knew was that this moment was one that would stick with him until the day he died.

He'd never forget the feel of Diana's softness in his hands, the way she looked at him as the city whirled past them in a blur of whirling silver light. Years from now, when he was nothing but a distant memory in her bewitching, beguiling mind, he'd remember what it had felt like to lose himself in that deep purple gaze. He'd close his eyes and dream of radiant blue light. God help him. He'd probably never be able to look at a sapphire again without getting hard.

"Diana, darling." He groaned and lowered his lips to her breasts, drawing a nipple into his mouth.

He was being too rough, and he knew it, nipping and biting with his teeth. But he couldn't stop. Not when she was arching toward his mouth and fisting her hands in his hair. His hunger was matched by her need, which didn't seem possible.

It was like falling into a mirror.

How will this end?

Badly. No question.

He couldn't fathom walking away from Diana Drake. But he knew he would. He always walked away. From everyone.

"Mr. Andrade." The driver's voice crackled over the intercom.

Franco ignored it and peeled Diana's dress lower. He was fully on top of her now, spread over the length of the backseat. He was kissing his way down her abdomen when the driver's voice came over the loud speaker again.

"Mr. Andrade, there are photographers at the end of the block, just outside the apartment building."

Diana stiffened beneath him.

"It's okay," he whispered. "Don't worry. Everything will be fine."

He gently lifted her dress back into place, cursing himself for being such an impatient idiot.

What were they doing? They weren't teenagers on prom night, for crying out loud. He was a grown man. The choices he made had consequences. And somehow the consequences of his involvement with Diana seemed to grow more serious by the day.

Diana sat up and brushed the chestnut bangs from her eyes. Her sapphire necklace shimmered in the dark.

Franco looked away and straightened his tie from the other end of the leather seat.

"We're here, Miss Drake, Mr. Andrade," the driver announced.

"Thank you," Franco said, squinting through the darkened car window.

The throng of paparazzi gathered at the entrance to the building was the largest he'd ever seen. The press attention was getting out of hand. The wedding would be a circus.

Get a grip.

He shook his head. There wasn't going to be a wedding. Ever. The engagement was a sham, despite the massive rock on Diana's finger.

The ring was messing with Franco's head. He was having enough trouble maintaining a grasp on reality, and seeing that diamond solitaire on Diana's hand every time she reached for him, touched him, stroked him just added to the confusion.

The back door opened, and he and Diana somehow managed to find their way inside the building amid the blinding light of flashbulbs. The photographers screamed questions at them about the details of the wedding. Would it be held at the Plaza? Who was designing Diana's wedding dress?

It occurred to Franco that he would have liked to see Diana dressed in bridal white. She would look stunning walking toward her man standing at the front of a church in front of the upper echelons of Manhattan society. A lucky man. A man who wasn't him.

They managed to keep their hands off each other as they navigated the route to Diana's front door. When had touching each other become something they did in private rather than for show? And why did that seem so dangerous when that's the way it should have always been?

Diana slid her key into the lock. She pushed the door open, and they paused at the threshold.

Franco caught her gaze and smiled. "I'm sorry about what happened in the car and the close call with the photographers. That was…" He shook his head, struggling for an appropriate adjective. *Careless. Intense. Fantastic.*

They all fit.

The corners of her perfect bow-shaped lips curved into a smile that could only be described as wicked. "I'm not sorry."

Franco swallowed. Hard.

Like falling into a mirror.

But mirrors broke when they fell. They ended up in tiny shards of broken glass that sparkled like diamonds but cut to the quick.

He didn't care what happened to him next month. Next week. Tomorrow. He just knew that before the night was over, he would bury himself inside Diana again. Consequences be damned.

The moment they stepped inside the apartment and the door clicked shut behind them, Diana found herself pressed against the wall. Franco's mouth was on hers in an instant, kissing her with such force, such need that her lips throbbed almost to the point of pain.

A forbidden thrill snaked its way through her. This was different than it had been the night before. They'd been somewhat cautious with each other then, neither of them willing to fully let down their guard. But she knew without having to ask that tonight wouldn't be like that. Tonight would be about surrender.

"Take off your dress," he ordered and took a step backward. His gaze settled on her sapphire necklace as he waited for her to obey.

She stood frozen, breathless for a moment, as she tried to make sense of what was happening. She shouldn't enjoy being told what to do, but this was for her pleasure. His. Theirs. And the molten warmth pooling in her center told her she liked it, indeed.

She reached behind her back for her zipper, but her hands were already shaking so hard that they were completely ineffectual. Franco moved closer, his face mere inches from hers. Her neck went hot, her knees buckled and she desperately wanted to look away. To take a deep breath and calm the frantic beating of her heart. But she couldn't seem to tear her gaze from his.

The corner of his mouth lifted into a barely visible half smile. His eyes blazed. He knew full well the effect he had on her. In moments like this, he owned her. He knew it, and so did she.

It should have frightened her. Diana had never wanted to belong to anyone, let alone him. And she wouldn't. Not once their charade was over and they'd gone their separate ways.

But just this once she wanted it to be true. Just for tonight.

"Turn around, love." His voice was raw, pained.

She did as he said and turned to face the wall. With excruciating care, he unzipped her gown. Red lace slid down her hips and fell to the floor. Franco's hands reached around to cup her breasts as his lips left a trail of tantalizing kisses down her spine.

"*Preciosa,*" he murmured against her bare back. *Lovely.*

His breath was like fire on her skin. She was shimmering, molten. A gemstone in the making.

She sighed and arched her back. Franco's hands slid from her breasts to her hips, where he hooked his fingers around her lacy panties and slid them down her legs. She stepped out of them, turned to face him, but he stopped her with a sharp command.

"No." He took her hands and pressed them flat against the wall, then whispered in her ear. "Don't move, Diana. Stay very still."

This was like nothing she'd ever experienced before. She'd never been with anyone besides Franco, but this was even different than the times they'd been together. The brush of his designer tuxedo against her exposed skin made her consciously aware of the fact that, once again, she was completely undressed while he remained fully clothed. She couldn't even see him, but that seemed to enhance the riot of sensations skittering through her body. She could only close her eyes and feel.

He brushed her hair aside and kissed her neck, her shoulder. His hands were everywhere—on her waist, her bottom, sliding over her belly. She was suddenly grateful for the wall and the way he'd pressed her hands against it. It was the only thing holding her up. Her legs had begun to tremble, and the tingle between them was almost too much to bear. She was so overwhelmed by the gentle assault of his mouth and the graceful exploration of his hands that she didn't even notice he'd nudged her legs apart with his knee until his fingertips reached between her thighs and found her center.

"I could touch you forever," he said and slid a finger inside her.

Forever.

It was a dangerous word, but this was a dangerous game they were playing. For all practical purposes, they were playing house. Living as husband and wife. And to Diana's astonishment, she didn't hate it.

On the contrary, she quite enjoyed it.

Especially now, bent over with Franco's fingers moving in and out of her. She moaned, low and delicious. She needed him to stop. Now, before she climaxed in this brazen posture. But she'd lost control of her body. Her hips were rocking in time with his hand, and she was opening herself up for him like a flower. A rare and beautiful orchid. Diamond white.

"Franco," she begged. "Please."

"Come," he whispered. "For me. Do it now."

Stars exploded before her eyes, falling like diamond dust as her body shuddered to its end. She collapsed into his arms, and he carried her across the apartment to the bedroom, whispering soothing words.

She'd gone boneless, yet her skin was alive. Shimmering like a glistening ruby. The King of Stones. And as he gingerly set her down and pushed inside her, she felt regal. Adored as no woman had ever been.

She was a queen, and Franco Andrade was her king.

Chapter Seventeen

Diana took her place at a reserved table situated near midfield, where Artem and Ophelia sat beneath the shade of a Drake-blue umbrella. She tried not to think too hard about the fact that this is what life would be like if she and Franco were together.

Really together.

Sundays at the Polo Club, sipping champagne with her brother and his wife, surrounded by the comforting scents of fresh-cut grass and cherry blossoms. A real family affair.

It wouldn't be so bad, would it?

Her throat grew tight. It felt quite nice, actually. Far too nice to be real.

Surrender.

It would have been so easy to give in. The past month had been more than business. It had been such a beautiful lie that she wondered sometimes if she actually believed it.

I could touch you forever.

Forever.

The word had branded itself on her skin, along with Franco's touch.

"Here he comes," Ophelia said.

Diana dragged her attention away from the night before and back to the present, where Franco was riding onto the field atop a beautifully muscled bay mare. The horse's dark tail was fashioned into a tight braid, and the bottoms of its legs were wrapped with bright red bandages. These were protective measures, necessary to guard against injury during play, rather than fashion statements. But the overall effect was striking just the same. The horse was magnificent.

But not as magnificent as its rider.

Diana had never seen Franco in full polo regalia before. Riding clothes, sure. But not like this...

He wore crisp white pants and brandy-colored boots that stretched all the way above his knees. The sleeves of his Kingsmen polo shirt strained at his biceps as he gave his mallet a few practice swings. She couldn't seem to stop looking at the muscles in his forearms. Or the way he carried himself in the saddle. Confident. Commanding. The aggressive glint in his eyes was just short of cocky.

He winked at her, and she realized he'd caught her staring. Before she could stop herself, she wiggled her white-gloved fingers in a tiny wave.

Beside her, Artem cleared his throat. "Are you ready for this, sis?"

She dropped her hand to her lap and nodded. "I am."

He was talking about the horses, of course. As far as Artem knew, she hadn't been this close to a horse since the day of her accident. She thought about telling him what Franco had done for her, but she couldn't find the words. She wasn't even sure words existed to describe what had happened when he'd taken her hands and placed them on the warmth of the gelding's back.

But the main reason she didn't try and explain was that she wanted to keep the grace of the moment to herself. To preserve its sanctity. Almost every move she and Franco had made for the past month had been splashed all over the newspapers. Every touch. Every kiss. Every lie. The truth between them lived in the quiet moments, the ones no one else had seen. And she wanted to keep it that way as long as she possibly could.

Because so long as no one knew how much he really meant to her, she could pretend the end didn't matter. She could hold her head high when the gossip pages screamed that she and Franco were over.

Right in front of her, the players were clustered together in the center of the field. The two teams faced each other, waiting for the throw-in—the moment when the umpire tossed the ball into play. Diana forced herself to watch, to concentrate on the present rather than what hadn't even happened yet. But as the bright white ball fell to the ground, she couldn't help but feel like time had begun to move at warp speed. And, with a resounding whack of Franco's mallet, it did.

The ball sailed across the grass, a startling white streak against bright, vivid green. Franco leaned into the saddle, and his horse charged forward. The ground shook beneath Diana's feet as the players charged toward the goal.

Franco led the charge, and when he hit the ball with such force that it went airborne, her heart leaped straight to her throat.

She held her breath while she waited for the official ruling. When the man behind the goal waved a flag over his head to indicate the Kingsmen had scored, she flew to her feet and cheered.

Franco caught her eye as his horse galloped toward the opposite end of the field. He smiled, and her head spun a little.

God, she was acting like an actual fiancée. A wife.

But she was supposed to, wasn't she? She was just doing her job.

It was more than that, though. There was no denying it. She wasn't acting at all.

Oh, no.

Her legs went wobbly, and she sank into her white wooden chair.

You're in love with him.

"He's amazing, isn't he?" Ophelia clapped and yelled Franco's name.

"He is, indeed." Diana felt sick.

How had she let this happen? Sleeping with Franco again—*twice*—had been stupid enough. Falling in love with him was another thing entirely. Off-the-charts idiotic.

The players flew past again in a flurry of galloping hooves and swinging mallets, and Diana's gaze remained glued to Franco. She shook her head and forced herself to look away, to concentrate on something real. The silver champagne bucket beside the table. The feathered hat situated at a jaunty angle on Ophelia's head. Anything. She counted to ten, but none of the little tricks she'd once used to stop herself from thinking about Diamond worked. She couldn't keep her eyes off Franco.

In the blink of an eye, he scored three more goals. It was a relief when the horn sounded, signaling the end of the first chukker. The break between periods was only three minutes, but she needed those three minutes. Every second of them. She needed a break from the intensity of the action on the field. Time to collect herself. Time to convince herself that she wasn't in love with the high-scoring player of the game.

Artem refilled their champagne flutes. "Franco's on fire today."

Diana watched him trot off the field toward a groom who stood by, ready and waiting, with Franco's next horse and mallet. By the time the match was finished, he'd go through at least seven horses. One for each chukker.

"Diana?" Artem slid a glass in front of her.

"Hmm?" she asked absently.

Franco had removed his helmet to rake his hand through his hair, a gesture that struck her as nonsensically sensual. Even from this distance.

"Could you peel your eyes away from your fiancé for half a second?" There was a smile in Artem's voice.

Sure enough, when she swiveled to face him, she found him grinning from ear to ear. Ophelia's chair was empty. Diana hadn't even noticed she'd left the table.

"Fake fiancé," she said. The back of her neck felt warm all of a sudden. She sipped her champagne and wished Artem would find something else to look at.

"You can stop now," Artem said. "I know."

"Know what?" But she was stalling. She knew exactly what he'd meant. He *knew*.

"About you and Andrade." His gaze flitted toward Franco climbing onto his new horse. This one was a sleek, solid-black gelding. Just like Diamond.

Diana's heart hammered in her chest. "Who told you?" Franco? Surely not.

But no one else knew.

"No one." Artem let out a laugh. "Are you kidding?

No one had to. I'm not blind, sis. It's written all over your face."

She shook her head. "No. We're not... I'm not..."

I'm not in love. I can't be.

"Don't even try to pretend it's an act. I'm not buying it this time." His gaze flitted from her to Franco and back again. "How long?"

Diana sighed. She was suddenly more exhausted than she'd ever been in her life. So many lies. She couldn't tell another one. Not to her brother. "I don't know when it happened, exactly."

Slowly. Yet, somehow, all at once.

Was it possible that she'd loved him all along, since the first night they'd been together, back when she was twenty-two?

"This is awful. Artem. What am I going to do?" She dropped her head into her hands.

Artem bent and whispered in her ear. "There are worse things in the world than falling for your fiancé."

She peered up at him from beneath the brim of her hat. "You seem to be forgetting the fact that we're not actually engaged. Also, I know for certain that you hate the thought of Franco and me."

His brow furrowed. "When exactly did I say that?"

She sat up straight and met his gaze. "The day of the Lamberti diamond announcement. And the morning the engagement was listed in the newspaper. And possibly a few other times over the course of the past four weeks."

He shook his head. "Clearly you weren't listening."

"Of course I was. You're not all that easy to ignore, my darling brother. Believe me, I've tried." She gave him a wobbly smile.

She felt like she was wearing her heart on the outside of her body all of a sudden. It terrified her to her core.

The giddy, bubbly feeling that came over her every time she looked at Franco was probably the same thing her mother had experienced when she'd looked at Diana's father. His long list of mistresses had no doubt felt the same way about him, too.

Fools, all of them.

Artem reached for her hand and gave it a squeeze. "I never said I didn't like the idea of you and Franco having a *genuine* relationship."

Could that be true? Because it wasn't the way she remembered their conversations. Then again, maybe she'd been the one who found the idea so repugnant, not Artem.

He leveled his gaze at her. "I was concerned about your pretend relationship. It seemed to be spinning out of control, far beyond what I intended when I make the mistake of suggesting it. But if it's real…"

If it's real.

That was the question, wasn't it?

She would have given anything in exchange for the answer.

Ophelia returned to the table as the next chukker began. Diana redirected her attention to the field, where Franco cut a dashing figure atop his striking black horse. Seconds after the toss-in, he was once again ahead of the other players, smacking the ball with his mallet and thundering toward the goal.

But just as he reached the far end of the field, a player from the other team cut diagonally between him and the ball.

"That's an illegal move," Artem said tersely.

Diana could hear Franco yelling in his native tongue. *Aléjate! Away!* But the player bore down and forced his horse directly in front of Franco's ebony gelding.

Somewhere a whistle sounded, but Diana barely heard

it. Her pulse had begun to roar in her ears as Franco and his horse got lost in the ensuing fray. She flew to her feet to try and get a better look. All she could see amid the tangle of horses, players and mallets was a flash of dazzling black.

Just like Diamond.

Her throat grew tight. She couldn't breathe. Couldn't speak. She reached for Artem, grabbed his forearm. The emerald grass seemed too bright all of a sudden. The sky, too blue. Garish. Like something out of a nightmare. And the black horse was a terrible omen.

No. She shook her head. *Please, no.*

There was a sickening thud, then everything stopped. There was no more noise. No more movement. Nothing.

Just the horrific sight of Franco lying facedown on top of that glaring green lawn. Motionless.

Franco heard his body break as it crashed into the ground. There was no mistaking the sound—an earsplitting crack that seemed as though it were echoing off the heavenly New York sky.

The noise was followed by a brutal pain dead in the center of his chest. It blossomed outward, until even his fingertips throbbed.

He squeezed his eyes closed and screamed into the grass.

Walk it off. It's nothing. You've been waiting for this chance for months. You can't get sidelined with an injury. Not now.

He moved. Just a fraction of an inch. It felt like someone had shot him through the left shoulder with a flame-tipped arrow. At least it wasn't his playing arm.

Still, it hurt like hell. He took a deep breath and rolled himself over with his right arm. He squeezed his eyes closed tight and muttered a stream of obscenities in Spanish.

"Don't move," someone said.

Not *someone*. Diana.

He opened his eyes, and there she was. Kneeling beside him in the grass. The wind lifted her hat, and it went airborne. She didn't seem to notice. She just stared down at him, wide-eyed and beautiful, as her dark hair whipped in the wind.

For a blissful moment, Franco forgot about his pain. He forgot everything but Diana.

If she was putting on an act, it was a damned convincing one. Something in his chest took flight, despite the pain.

"You're a sight for sore eyes, you know that?" He winced. Talking hurt. Breathing hurt. Everything hurt.

Especially the peculiar way Diana was looking at him. As if she'd seen a ghost. "Why are you sitting up? You shouldn't be moving."

"And you shouldn't be on the field. You're going to get hurt." She was on her hands and knees in the grass, too close to the horses' hooves. Too ghastly pale. Too upset.

She remembers.

He could see it in the violet depths of her eyes—the agony of memory.

"*I'm* going to get hurt? Look at you, Franco. You *are* hurt." She peered up at the other riders. "Someone do something. Get a doctor. Call an ambulance. Please."

Luc had already dismounted and stood behind her with the reins to his horse as well as Franco's in his hand. He passed the horses off to one of their other teammates and knelt beside Diana. "The medics are coming, Diana. Help is on its way. He's fine. See?"

She blinked and appeared to look right through him.

Franco wished he knew what was going on in her head. Which part of her horrific accident was she remembering?

He'd known she was having trouble coming to terms with what had happened to her…with what had happened to Diamond. But he'd never once suspected that she remembered her accident. She'd had a concussion. She'd been unconscious. Those memories should have been mercifully lost.

No wonder she'd had such a hard time moving on.

"Diana, look at me." He reached for her, and a hot spike of pain shot through his shoulder. He cursed and used his right arm to hold the opposite one close to his chest.

A collarbone fracture. He would have bet money on it.

It was a somewhat serious injury, but not the worst thing in the world. With any luck he'd be back on the field in four weeks. Six, tops.

But he didn't care about that right now. All he cared about was the woman kneeling beside him…the things she remembered…the fear shining in her luminous eyes.

He'd been such an idiot.

The list of things he'd done wrong was endless. He shouldn't have pushed her to overcome her fears. He shouldn't have ridden a jet-black horse today. He damn well shouldn't have pressured her into watching him play.

He wished he could go back in time and change the things he'd said, the things he'd done. He would have given anything to make that happen. He'd never set foot on a polo field again if it meant he could turn back the clock.

If that were possible—if he could step back in time, he'd walk…run…all the way to the first moment he'd touched her. Not last night. Not last week.

Three years ago.

"Diana, I'm fine. Everything is fine."

But his assurances were lost in the commotion as the medical team reached him. He was surrounded by medics, shouting instructions and cutting his shirt open so they could assess his injuries. Someone shone a light in his eyes. When the spots disappeared from his vision, he could see the game officials clearing the horses and riders away. Giving him space.

He couldn't see Diana anymore. Suddenly, people were everywhere. Jack Ellis loomed over him, his expression grave. The emergency medical team was carrying a stretcher out onto the field.

Franco looked up at Ellis. "Is all of this really necessary? It's a collarbone. I'll be fine."

"Let's hope so," Ellis said coldly. "We need you on the tour."

Luc cleared his throat. His gaze fixed on Franco's, and Franco felt...

Nothing.

For months this was all he'd wanted. Polo was his life. Since he'd left home at eleven, he'd lived and breathed it. Without it, he'd been lost. The thought of losing it again, even for a few weeks, combined with the look on Ellis's face should have filled him with panic.

He wasn't sure what to make of the fact that it didn't.

"Diana," he said, ignoring Ellis and focusing instead on Luc. "Where is she? Where did she go?"

"She's with her brother." Luc jerked his head in the direction of the reserved tables.

"Go find her." Franco winced. The pain was getting worse. "Bring her to the hospital. Please."

Luc nodded. "The second the game is over, I will."

The game.

Franco had all but forgotten about the scrimmage. He'd turned his life upside down to get back on the team, and in a matter of seconds it no longer mattered.

Slow down. This is your life. She's a Drake. You're not. Remember?

Diana would be fine.

She was a champion. She'd come so far in conquering her fears in recent weeks. She was close. So close. His fall had been nothing like hers. Of course she'd been rattled, but by the time he saw her again, she'd be okay.

He clung to that belief as the paramedics strapped him to a stretcher and lifted him into an ambulance.

But the look on Diana's face when she walked into his hospital room however many hours later hurt Franco more than his damned arm did. The person standing at his bedside was a ghost of the woman he'd taken to bed the night before. Memories moved in the depths of her amethyst eyes.

Painful remembrance.

And stone-cold fear.

Franco had seen that look before in the eyes of spooked horses. Horses that had been through hell and back, and flinched at even the gentlest touch. It took years of patience and tender handling to get those horses to trust a man again. Sometimes they never did.

"You're here." He shifted on the bed, and a spike of pain shot from his wrist to his shoulder. But he didn't dare flinch. "I'm glad you came."

She gave him an almost invisible smile. "Of course I came. I'm your fiancée, remember? How would it look if I weren't here?"

So they'd gone from making love to just keeping up appearances. Again. Marvelous.

"Sweetheart." He reached for her hand and forced himself to speak with a level of calmness that was in direct contrast to the panic blossoming in his chest. "It's not as bad as it looks. I promise."

She nodded wordlessly, but when she quietly removed her hand from his, the gesture spoke volumes. He was losing her. It couldn't happen again. He wouldn't let it, damn it. Not this time. Not for good.

"Diana..."

"I'm fine." There was that forced smile again. "Honestly."

He didn't believe her for a minute, and he wasn't in the mood to pretend he did. Hadn't they been pretending long enough? "You're not fine, Diana."

She stared at him until the pain in her gaze hardened. *Go ahead, get mad. Just feel something, love. Anything.* "Be real with me."

She shook her head. "We had an agreement, Franco."

"Screw our agreement." She flinched as if he'd slapped her. "There's more here than a fake love affair. We both know there is."

"Stop." She exhaled a ragged breath. "Please stop. The gala is in two days, and so is the Kingsmen tour."

"Do I look like I'm in any kind of condition to play polo right now?" He threw off the covers and climbed out of the hospital bed. There was too much at stake in this conversation to have it lying down.

"You're going on the tour. Luc said Ellis is insisting that you come along. As soon as your injury heals, you'll be right back in the saddle." Her gaze shifted to his splint, and she swallowed. Hard.

"I'll always ride. It's not just my job. It's my life." Using his good arm, he reached to cup her cheek. When she didn't pull away, it felt like a minor victory. "It's yours, too, Diana. That's one of the things that makes us so good together. You'll ride again. You will. When you're ready, and I intend to be there when it happens."

She backed out of his reach. So much for small victories. The space between them suddenly felt like an impossibly vast gulf. "Go on tour, Franco. You'll be fired again if you don't."

Franco sighed. "I highly doubt that."

"It's true. Ask Luc. Apparently your coach wants to keep an eye on you." Her gaze narrowed. "I guess he doesn't want to leave you behind with his wife."

Shit. That again.

"Natalie Ellis means nothing to me, Diana. She never did."

"That's not such a nice way to talk about a woman you slept with. A woman who was *married*, I might add."

Franco followed her gaze to her ring finger, where her Drake Diamonds engagement ring twinkled beneath the fluorescent hospital lighting. He watched, helpless, as she slid it off her hand.

No. Every cell in his body screamed in protest. "What do you think you're doing?"

"I'm breaking up with you." She opened her handbag and dropped the ring inside. Her gaze flitted around the room. She seemed to be looking anywhere and everywhere but at him.

"Why remove the ring? It's not as if I actually gave it to you." Would she have been able to remove it so easily if he had?

He hoped not, but he couldn't be sure.

"I still think it's a good idea to take it off. You know, in case the press…"

"You think I still give a damn what the press thinks? Here's a headline for you—I don't. This isn't about our agreement. It's not about Drake Diamonds or Natalie

Ellis. It sure as hell isn't about the press. What's happening in this room is about you and me, Diana. No one else."

He'd fallen off his horse—something he'd done countless times before with varying degrees of consequences. Over the course of his riding career, he'd broken half a dozen bones and survived three concussions. But never before had a fall caused so much pain.

"Diana, you're afraid. But I'm fine. I promise. Now stop this nonsense. We have a gala to attend in two days."

She shook her head. "We had a deal, and now it's over. We both got what we wanted. It's time to walk away."

"Don't do this, Wildfire." His voice broke, but he couldn't have cared less. The only thing he cared about was changing her mind.

He wasn't sure when, but somewhere along the way he'd stopped pretending. He had feelings for Diana Drake. Feelings he had no intention of walking away from.

"Marry me."

Her face went pale. "You're not serious."

"I am. Quite." He'd never wanted this. Never asked for it. But he did now. The future suddenly seemed crystal clear.

She saw it, too. He knew she did. She could close her eyes as tightly as she wanted, but it was still there. Diamond bright.

"I'll marry you right now. We could go straight to the hospital chapel. Just say yes." They could have a fancy ceremony later on. Or not. Franco didn't care. He just wanted to be with her for the rest of his life. "Come on the tour with me, Diana. I don't want to do this without you."

"No." She shook her head. "You're not. You're just confused. I am, too. But it's not real. *We're* not real. You know that as well as I do."

"All I know is that I'm in love with you, Diana."

"Is that what you told Natalie Ellis? Were you in love with her too?" Diana's gaze narrowed. "You slept with a married woman, Franco. Your boss's wife. Do you even believe in marriage?"

What was he supposed to say to that?

I never slept with her.

I lied.

She'd never believe him. "There's never been anyone else, Diana. Only you."

"That doesn't exactly answer my question, does it? I can't marry you, Franco. Don't you see that? I might be a Drake, but I'm not my mother. She stood by the man she loved, even as he slept with every other woman who crossed his path. It killed her. It would kill me, too."

Then Diana turned and walked right out the door, and Franco was left with only the devastating truth.

He knew nothing.

Nothing at all.

Chapter Eighteen

The Met Diamond gala was supposed to be the most triumphant moment of Diana's fledgling career as a jewelry executive, but she dreaded it with every fiber of her being. She should have been walking up the museum's legendary steps on Franco's arm. She couldn't face the possibility of doing so alone. Not when every paparazzo in the western hemisphere would be there, wondering what had happened to her famous fiancé. She'd rather ride naked through the streets of Manhattan, Lady Godiva-style. But she'd made a promise, and she intended to honor it.

Thank God for Artem and Ophelia. Not only did they ride with her in the Drake limo, but they also flanked her as she climbed the endless marble staircase. She didn't know what she would have done without them. Artem slipped her arm through his and effectively held her upright as she was assaulted by thousands of flashbulbs and an endless stream of questions.

"Diana, where's Franco?"

"When's the wedding?"

"Don't tell us there's trouble in paradise!"

She wanted to clamp her hands over her ears. She could hear the photographers shouting even after they'd made it inside the museum.

"Are you okay?" Artem eyed her with concern.

God, she loved her brother. This night was every bit as important for him as it was for her, but his first concern was her broken heart.

She forced a smile and lied through her teeth. "I'm fine."

"No, you're not," Ophelia whispered. "You're shaking like a leaf. Artem, call our driver back. Diana should go home."

As good as that sounded, she couldn't. She'd made it this far. Surely she could last another few hours. Besides, she couldn't hide forever. The world would find out about her breakup eventually. It was time to face the music.

She was shocked no one had learned the truth yet. Two days had passed since she'd ended things with Franco. He hadn't breathed a word to the press, apparently. Which left her more confused than ever.

"Diana, I'd like you to stay." Artem glanced at his watch. "At least for half an hour. Then you can go straight home. Okay?"

"Artem…" Ophelia implored.

He cast a knowing glance in his wife's direction, one of those secret signals that spouses used to communicate. Diana would never be on the receiving end of such a look. Obviously.

"Thirty minutes," he repeated. "That's all I'm asking."

"No problem. I told you I'm fine, and I meant it." For the thousandth time since she'd walked out the door of

Franco's hospital room, the pad of her thumb found the empty spot where her engagement ring used to be.

A lump sprang to her throat.

She wasn't fine. She hadn't been fine since the moment she'd seen Franco fall to the ground at the polo match.

She'd thought she'd been ready to be around horses again, but she hadn't. She'd thought she'd been ready for a real relationship, one that might possibly lead to a *real* engagement and a *real* marriage, but she'd been wrong about that, too.

She couldn't lose anyone again. She'd lost both her mother and her father, and she'd lost Diamond. Enough was enough. She couldn't marry Franco. Not now. Not ever. If she did and something happened to him—if she lost him, too—she'd never be able to recover.

She shouldn't even want to marry him, anyway. The man had zero respect for the sanctity of marriage. He'd been fired for sleeping with his boss's wife, which meant that Diana had somehow fallen for a man who was exactly like her dad.

She'd have to be insane to accept his proposal.

Even though she'd almost wanted to...

"Excuse me." A familiar voice broke into their trio.

Diana turned to find the last person in the world she ever expected to see. "Luc?"

What on earth was Luc Piero doing at the Met Diamond gala? Had Franco not even told his closest friend that the engagement was off?

"Luc, I'm sorry. There's been a change of plans. Franco's not with me tonight." *Or any other night.*

He shook his head. "I'm not here for Franco. I came to talk to you."

"Me?" She swallowed.

What could she and Luc possibly have to talk about?

"Yes. You." He looked around at their posh surroundings. The Met was stunning on any given day, but tonight was special. Faux diamonds dripped from every surface. It was like standing inside a chandelier. "Is there someplace more private where we can chat?"

She shouldn't leave. She had a job to do. She had to speak to the Lambertis and pose for photos. And just looking at Luc made her all the more aware of how much she missed Franco.

She shook her head, but at the same time she heard herself agreeing. "Come with me." She glanced at Artem and Ophelia, who'd been watching the exchange with blatant curiosity. "I'll be right back."

She led Luc past the spot where the Lamberti diamond, which had just been officially rechristened the Lamberti-Drake diamond, glowed in a spectacular display case in the center of the Great Hall. Her stilettos echoed on the smooth tile floor as they rounded the corner beneath one of the Met's sweeping marble archways. When they reached the darkened hall of Greek and Roman art, her footsteps slowed to a stop.

They were alone here, in the elegant stillness of the sculpture collection. Gods and goddesses carved from stone surrounded them on every side. Secret keepers.

Diana was so tired of secrets. She'd spent her entire life mired in them. No one outside the family knew the circumstances surrounding her mother's death. Diana hadn't been allowed to talk about it. Nor did the public know the identity of Artem's biological mother. To the outside world, the Drakes were perfect.

So much deception. When would it end?

She turned to face Luc. "What is it? Has something happened to him?"

She hadn't realized how afraid she'd been until she uttered the words aloud.

Luc wouldn't have sought her out if what he had to say wasn't important. The moment he'd asked to speak to her in private, her thoughts had spun in a terrible direction. She remembered what it had felt like to find her mother's lifeless body on the living room floor...the panic that had shaken her to her core. It had been the worst moment of her life. Worse than her accident. Worse than losing Diamond. Worse than watching Franco's body break.

Every choice she'd made since the day her mother died had been carefully orchestrated so she'd never feel that way again. And where had it gotten her?

Completely and utterly alone.

But that wasn't so bad. She could handle loneliness. What she couldn't handle was the way her heart had broken in two the moment she'd seen Franco's lifeless body on the ground.

She'd fought her love for him. She'd fought it hard. But she'd fallen, all the same.

"No, he's fine." Luc's brow furrowed. "Physically, I mean. But he's not fine. Not really. That's why I'm here."

Her heart gave a little lurch. "Oh?"

Franco couldn't possibly love her. Not after the way she'd treated him. He'd been real with her. Unflinchingly, heart-stoppingly real. And she'd refused to do the same.

Worse, she'd judged him. Time and again. She'd acted so self-righteously, when all along they'd both been doing the same thing—running from the past. She'd chosen solitude, and in a way, so had Franco. Neither one of them had let anyone close. Until the day Franco asked her to marry him.

He was ready to leave the past behind. He was moving

beyond it, and he'd offered to do so hand in hand with Diana. But she'd turned him down.

She'd spent years judging him, and now she knew why. Not because the things he'd done were unforgivable, but because it was convenient. So long as she believed him to be despicable, he couldn't hurt her.

Or so she'd thought.

But he hadn't hurt her, had he? She'd hurt herself. She'd hurt them both.

"He's in love with you, Diana," Luc said.

She shook her head. "I don't think so."

She'd made sure of that.

"You're wrong. I've known Franco all his life, and I've never seen him like this before." The gravity in his gaze brought a pang to her chest. "He misses you."

She shook her head. "Stop. *Please.*"

Why was he doing this? She'd nearly made it. Franco was leaving with the Kingsmen in less than twenty-four hours. Once he was gone, she'd have no choice but to put their mockery of a romance behind her and move on. She just had to hold on for one more day.

A single, heartbreaking day.

She swallowed. "I'm sorry, Luc. But I can't hear this. Not now."

She needed to get out of here. She'd thought she could turn up in a pretty gown and smile for the cameras one last time, but she couldn't. All she wanted to do was climb into bed with her dog and a pint of ice cream.

She gathered the skirt of ball gown in her hands and tried to slip past Luc, but he blocked her exit. He jammed his hands on his hips, and his expression turned tortured. "You're going to make me say it, aren't you?"

Diana was afraid to ask what he was talking about. Terrified to her core. She couldn't take any more. Refusing Franco had been the most difficult thing she'd ever had to do.

But she couldn't quite bring herself to ignore the torment in Luc's gaze. "I don't know what you're talking about."

Luc shook his head. "Franco is going to kill me. But you deserve to know the truth."

The truth.

A chill ran up Diana's spine. She had the sudden urge to clasp her hands over her ears.

But she'd been turning her back on the truth long enough, hadn't she?

No more secrets. No more lies.

"What is it?" Her voice shook. And when Luc turned his gaze on her with eyes filled with regret, she had to bite down hard on the inside of her cheek to keep from crying.

His gaze dropped to the floor, where shadows of gods and goddesses stretched across the museum floor in cool blue hues. "Look, I don't know what happened between the two of you, but there's something you should know."

Diana nodded wordlessly. She didn't trust herself to speak. She couldn't even bring herself to look at him. Instead, she focused on the marble sculpture directly behind him. Cupid's alabaster wings stretched toward the sky as he bent to revive Psyche with a kiss.

A tear slid down her cheek.

"Tell me," she whispered, knowing full well there would be no turning back from this moment.

Luc fixed his gaze with hers. The air in the room grew still. Even the sculptures seemed to hold their breath.

"It was me," he said.

Diana began to shake from head to toe. She wrapped

her arms around herself in an effort to keep from falling apart. "Luc, what are you saying?"

"I was the one who had an affair with Ellis's wife, not Franco." He blinked a few times, very quickly. His eyes went red, until he stood looking at Diana through a shiny veil of tears. "I'm sorry."

Diana shook her head. "No."

She wanted him to take the words back. To swallow them up as if she'd never heard them.

"No!" Her voice echoed off the tile walls.

Luc held up his hands in a gesture of surrender. "It wasn't my idea. It was Franco's. I left my Kingsmen championship ring in Ellis's bed. He found it and knew it belonged to one of the players. Franco confessed before I could stop him."

"I can't believe what I'm hearing." But on some level, she could.

Franco loved Luc like a brother. He wanted to protect him, just as Luc had protected him when he'd been living in his barn and then his home.

She should have figured it out. From the very beginning, she'd suspected there was more to Franco's termination than he'd admitted. Then, at Argentine Night at the Polo Club, Natalie Ellis had looked right through him.

And Diana had known.

Franco had never touched her.

But Diana had been so ready to believe the worst about him, she'd pushed her instincts aside. What had she done?

"He never anticipated being cut from the team. He was too valuable. But Ellis couldn't stand the sight of him. I tried to tell the truth. Over and over again. Franco wouldn't have it."

She wanted to pound her fists against his chest. She wanted to scream. *You should have tried harder.*

But she didn't. Couldn't. Because deep down, she was just as guilty as he was. Guilty of letting the past color the way she saw her future.

I should have believed.

Franco wasn't her father. Loving him didn't make her into her mother. And she *did* love him, despite her best efforts not to.

She'd spent every waking second since her accident trying to protect herself from experiencing loss again, and it had happened anyway. She'd fallen in love with Franco, and she'd lost him. Because she'd pushed him away.

"Tell me this changes things." Luc searched her gaze. His eyes were red rimmed, but they held a faint glimmer of hope.

"I wish it could." Her heart felt like it was going to pound out of her chest. She pressed the heel of her hand against her breastbone, but it didn't make a difference. She was choking on her remorse. "He asked me to marry him, Luc. And I turned him down."

Luc's brow furrowed. "What do you mean? I thought you were already engaged. It was in all the papers."

"He didn't tell you?" Her voice broke, and her heart broke along with it. "It was never real."

"He never said a word."

The fact that Franco never told Luc their relationship was a sham meant something. Diana wasn't sure what… but it did. It had to. He'd been willing to sacrifice everything for Luc, but he'd let his closest friend believe he was in love. He'd let him think he was going to marry her.

And that made whatever they'd had seem more genuine than Diana had ever allowed herself to believe.

It was real. It had been real all along.

She needed to go to him. What was she doing standing here while he was preparing to leave? "Sorry Luc, there's something I need to do."

She turned and ran out of the sculpture gallery, her organza dress swishing around her legs as she ran toward the foyer. But when she rounded the corner, she collided hard against the solid wall of someone's chest.

A hard, sculpted chest.

She'd know that chest anywhere.

"Franco, you're here." She pulled back to look up at him, certain she was dreaming.

She wasn't. It was him. He was wincing and holding his arm in the sling where she'd banged against it, but it was him. She'd never been so happy to see an injured man in all her life.

"I am." He smiled, and if her heart hadn't already been broken, it would have split right in two.

It felt like a century had passed since she'd walked out of his hospital room. A century in which she'd convinced herself she'd never see him again. Never get to tell him the things she should have said when she'd had the chance...

"Franco, there's something I need to say." She took a deep breath. "I'll go with you on tour. Please take me with you."

His smile faded ever so slightly. "Diana..."

"I just want to be with you, Franco. *Really* be with you." She choked back a sob. "If you'll still have me."

She felt as if she'd just taken her broken heart and given it to him as an offering. Such vulnerability should have made her panic. But it was far easier than she'd expected. Natural. Right. The only thing making her panic was the thought that she'd almost let him leave Manhattan without telling him how she felt.

She took a deep, shuddering inhale and said the words

she'd tried all her life not to say. "I love you. I always have. Take me with you."

Around them, partygoers glided in the silvery light. The air sparkled with diamond dust. They could have been standing in the middle of a fairy tale.

But as Franco's smile wilted, Diana plunged headfirst into a nightmare.

"It's too late." He took her hands in his, but he was shaking his head and his gaze was filled with apologies that she didn't want to hear.

She'd missed her chance.

She should have believed.

She should have said yes when she'd had the opportunity.

"I understand." She pulled her hands away and began gathering her skirt in her fists, ready to run for the door. Just like Cinderella.

The ball was over.

Everything was over.

"It's okay." But it wasn't. It would never be okay, and it was all her fault. "I just really need to go…"

"Diana, wait." Franco stepped in front of her. "Please."

She couldn't do this. Not now. Not here, with all of New York watching. Couldn't he understand that?

But she'd fallen in love while the world watched. She supposed there was some poetic symmetry to having her heart broken while the cameras rolled.

"I can't." It was too much. More than she could take. More than anyone could.

But just as she turned away, Franco blurted, "I quit the team."

Diana stopped. She released her hold on her dress, and featherlight organza floated to the floor. "What?"

"That's what I meant when I said it's too late. You

can't go with me on the road because I'm not going." His mouth curved into a half grin, and Diana thought she might faint. "Did you really think I could leave you?"

He's not my father.

She'd turned him down, sent him away. And he was still here. He'd stuck by Luc, even when it had come at great personal cost.

Now he was sticking by her. He was loyal in a way she'd never known could be possible.

"You're afraid," he said in a deliciously low tone that she felt deep in her center. "Don't be."

He moved closer, cupped her face with his left hand. She'd missed him. She'd missed his touch. So, so much. She could have wept with relief at the feel of his warm skin against hers.

"I'm not afraid. Not anymore." She searched his gaze for signs of doubt, but found only rock-solid assurance. His eyes glittered, as sharp as diamonds.

He dropped his hand, and her fingertips drifted to her cheek, to the place where he'd touched her. She hadn't wanted him to release her. *Too soon*, she thought. She needed his hands on her. His lips. His tongue.

Everywhere.

"Wildfire." Franco winked, and she felt it down to the toes of her silver Jimmy Choos. "I have something for you."

He reached into the inside pocket of his tuxedo and pulled out a tiny Drake-blue box tied with a white satin ribbon. It was just like the ones she'd once sold to all the moonstruck couples in Engagements.

Diana stared at it, trying to make sense of what was happening. For as long as she could remember, she'd hated those boxes. But not this time.

This time, the tears that pricked her eyes were tears of joy.

"Franco, what are you doing?" How had he even gotten that box? Or whatever was inside of it?

Her gaze flitted over Franco's shoulder, and she spotted Artem watching from afar with a huge grin on his face. So her brother was in on this, too? That would certainly explain where the tiny blue box had come from. It also explained his insistence that she stay for the beginning of the gala.

Is this really happening?

"Isn't it obvious what I'm doing?" Franco dropped down on one knee, right there in the Great Hall of the Met.

It *was* happening.

A gasp went up from somewhere in the crowd as the partygoers noticed Franco's posture. Diana could hear them murmuring in confusion. Of course they were baffled. She and Franco were supposed to be engaged already.

Let them be confused. For once, Diana didn't care what anyone was saying about her. She didn't care what kind of headlines would be screaming from the front page of the papers tomorrow morning. All she cared about was the man kneeling at her feet.

"It occurred to me that I never asked properly for you to become to my wife. Not the way in which you deserve. So I'm giving it another go." He took her hand and gently placed the blue box in it.

Her fingertips closed around it, and their eyes met. Held.

"I love you, Diana Drake. Only a fool would walk away from something real, and I don't want to be a fool anymore. So I'm asking you again, and I'm going to keep asking for as long as it takes." But there would be no more proposals, because she was going to say yes. She could barely keep herself from screaming her answer before he finished. *Yes, yes, yes.* "Will you marry me, Diana Drake?"

"I'd love to marry you, Franco Andrade."

The crowd cheered as he rose to his feet and took her into his arms. Diana was barely conscious of the popping of a champagne cork or the well-wishers who offered their congratulations. She was only aware of how right it felt to be by Franco's side again and how the tiny blue box in her hand felt like a magic secret.

She waited to open it until they were back at her apartment. The time between his proposal and the end of the party passed in a glittering blur. She needed to be alone with him. She needed to step out of her fancy dress and give herself to him, body and soul.

After they left the gala and finally arrived at her front door, Diana wove her fingers through Franco's and pulled him inside.

"Alone at last," he said, gazing down at her as the lights of Manhattan twinkled behind him.

"Sort of." Diana laughed and lifted a brow at Lulu, charging at them from the direction of the bedroom.

Franco scooped the puppy into the elbow of his uninjured arm and sat down on the sofa. Lulu burrowed into his lap, and he gave the empty space beside him a pat. "Come sit down. Don't you have a box to open?"

She sat and removed the little blue box from her evening bag. She held it in the palm of her hand, not wanting the moment to end. She wanted to hoard her time with Franco like a priceless treasure. Every precious second.

"Open it, Wildfire."

She tugged on the smooth satin ribbon and it fell onto her lap, where Lulu pounced on it with her tiny black paws. As the puppy picked it up with her mouth, she fell over onto her back between them, batting at the ribbon with her feet. The comical sight brought a lump to Diana's throat for some strange reason.

Then she realized why...

The three of them were a family.

She lifted the lid of the box, but the large rose-cut diamond solitaire nestled on top of the tiny Drake-blue cushion inside was unlike any of the rings in the shiny cases of the Engagements section of Drake Diamonds. Jewelers didn't typically style diamonds in rose cut anymore. This ring was different. Special. Familiar in a way that stole the breath from Diana's lungs.

"This was my mother's ring." She hadn't seen this diamond in years, but she would have recognized it anywhere. When she was a little girl, she used to slip it on and dream about the day when she'd wear sparkling diamonds and go to fancy black-tie parties every night, just as her parents did.

That had been in the years before everything turned pear-shaped. Before they'd all learned the truth about her father and his secret family. Back when being a wife and a mother seemed like a wonderful thing to be.

Diana had forgotten what it was like to feel that way.

Now, with breathless clarity, she remembered.

"How did you get this, Franco?" It was more than a stone. It was hope and happiness, shining bright. Diamond fire.

"I went to Artem to ask for your hand, and he gave it to me. He said it's been in the vault at Drake Diamonds for years. Waiting." Franco took the ring and slid it onto her finger. Then he lifted her hand and kissed her fingertips.

The diamond had been waiting all this time. Waiting for her broken heart to heal. Waiting for the one man who could help her put it back together.

Waiting for Franco.

At long last, the wait was over.

Epilogue

A *Page Six* Exclusive Report

Diamond heiress Diana Drake returns to New York today after winning a gold medal in equestrian show jumping at the Tokyo Olympics. The win is a shocking comeback after Drake suffered a horrific fall last year in Bridgehampton that resulted in the death of her beloved horse, Diamond. Drake's new mount—a Hanoverian mare named Sapphire—was a gift from her husband, polo-playing hottie Franco Andrade.

Andrade was on hand in Tokyo to watch his wife win the gold, where we hear there was plenty of Olympic-level PDA. We can't get enough of Manhattan's most beautiful power couple, so *Page Six* will be front row center this weekend when Andrade returns to the polo field as captain of the newly formed team, Black Diamond, which he co-owns with his longtime friend and teammate, Luc Piero.

All eyes will certainly be on Diana, who is returning to the helm of her family's empire Drake Diamonds as co-CEO. Rumor has it she declined a glass of champagne at the party celebrating her Olympic victory, and we can't help but wonder…

Might there be a baby on the horizon for this golden couple?

Only time will tell.

* * * * *

Love finds the Drake siblings in the glittering world of jewels and New York City.

If you enjoy IT STARTED WITH A DIAMOND, be sure to check out the first two books in the **DRAKE DIAMONDS** *series,* **HIS BALLERINA BRIDE** *and* **THE PRINCESS PROBLEM** *wherever Harlequin Special Edition books and ebooks are sold.*

www.Harlequin.com

Katrina Bailey's life is at a crossroads, so when arrogant—but sexy—Bowie Callahan asks for her help caring for his newly discovered half brother, she accepts, never expecting it to turn into something more...

Read on for a sneak peek at SERENITY HARBOR, the next book in the HAVEN POINT series by New York Times *bestselling author RaeAnne Thayne available July 2017!*

CHAPTER ONE

"THAT'S HIM AT your six o'clock, over by the tomatoes. Brown hair, blue eyes, ripped. Don't look. Isn't he *gorgeous*?"

Katrina Bailey barely restrained from rolling her eyes at her best friend. "How am I supposed to know that if you won't let me even sneak a peek at the man?" she asked Samantha Fremont.

Sam shrugged with another sidelong look in the man's direction. "Okay. You can look. Just make it subtle."

Mere months ago, all vital details about her best friend's latest crush might have been the most fascinating thing the two of them talked about all week. Right now, she found it tough to work up much interest in one more man in a long string of them, especially with everything else she had spinning in her life right now.

She wanted to ignore Sam's request and continue on with shopping for the things they needed to take to Wynona's shower—but friends didn't blow off their friends' obsessions. She loved Sam and had missed hanging out with her over the last nine months. It made her sad that their interests appeared to have diverged so dramatically, but it wouldn't hurt her to act like she cared about the cute newcomer to Haven Point.

Donning her best ninja spy skills—honed from years of doing this very thing, checking out hot guys without them noticing—she pretended to reach up to grab a can of peas off the shelf. She studied the label intently, all while shifting her gaze toward the other end of the aisle.

About ten feet away, she spotted two men. Considering she knew Darwin Twitchell well—and he was close to eighty years old and cranky as a badger with gout—the other guy had to be Bowie Callahan, the new director of research and development at the Caine Tech facility in town.

Years of habit couldn't be overcome by sheer force of will. That was the only reason her stomach muscles seemed to shiver and her toes curled against the leather of her sandals. Or so she told herself, anyway.

Okay. She got it. Sam was totally right. The man was indeed great-looking: tall, lean, tanned, with sculpted features and brown hair streaked with the sort of blond highlights that didn't come from a salon but from spending time outside.

Under other circumstances, she might have wanted to do more than look. In a different life, perhaps she would have made her way to his end of the aisle, pretended to fumble with an item on the shelf, then dropped it right at his feet so they could "meet" while they both reached to pick it up.

She used to be such an idiot.

The old Katrina might not have been able to look away from such a gorgeous male specimen. But when he aimed a ferocious scowl downward, she shifted her gaze to find him frowning at a boy who looked to be about five or six, trying his best to put a box of sugary cereal into their cart and growing visibly upset when Bowie Callahan kept taking it out and putting it back on the shelf.

Katrina frowned. "You didn't say he had a kid. I thought you had a strict rule. No divorced dads."

"He doesn't have a kid!" Sam exclaimed.

"Then who's the little kid currently winding up for what looks like a world-class tantrum at his feet?"

Ignoring her own stricture about not staring, Sam whirled around. Her eyes widened with confusion. "I have no idea! I heard it straight from Eliza Caine that he's not married and doesn't have a family. He never said anything to me about a kid when I met him at a party at Snow Angel Cove or the other two times I've bumped into him around town this spring. I haven't seen him around for a few weeks. Maybe he has family visiting. Or maybe he's babysitting or something."

That was so patently ridiculous, Katrina had to bite her tongue. Really? Did Sam honestly believe the new director of research and development at Caine Tech would be offering babysitting services—in the middle of the day and on a Monday, no less?

She sincerely adored Samantha for a million different reasons, but sometimes her friend saw what she wanted to see.

This latest example of how their paths had diverged in recent months made her a little sad. Until a year ago, she and Sam had been—as her mom would say—two peas of the same pod. They shared the same taste in music, movies, clothes. They could spend hours poring over celebrity and fashion magazines, dishing about the latest gossip, shopping for bargains at thrift stores and yard sales.

And men. She didn't even want to think about how many hours of her life she had wasted with Sam, talking about whichever guy they were most interested in that day.

Samantha had been her best friend since they found each other in junior high in that mysterious way like discovered like.

She still loved her dearly. Sam was kind and generous and funny, but Katrina's own priorities had shifted. After the events of the last year, Katrina was beginning to realize she barely resembled the somewhat shallow, flighty girl she had been before she grabbed her passport and hopped on a plane with Carter Ross.

That was a good thing, she supposed, but she felt a little pang of fear that while on the path to gaining a little maturity, she might end up losing her best friend.

"Babysitting. I suppose it's possible," she said in a noncommittal voice. If so, the guy was really lousy at it. The boy's face had reddened, and tears had started streaming down his features. By all appearances, he was approaching a meltdown, and Bowie Callahan's scowl had shifted to a look of helpless frustration.

"If you want, I can introduce you," Sam said, apparently oblivious to the drama.

Katrina purposely pushed their cart forward, in the opposite direction. "You know, it doesn't look like a good time. I'm sure I'll have a chance to meet him later. I'll be in Haven Point for a month. Between Wyn's wedding and Lake Haven Days, there should be plenty of time to socialize with our newest resident."

"Are you sure?" Sam asked, disappointment clouding her gaze.

"Yeah. Let's just finish shopping so I have time to go home and change before the shower."

Not that her mother's house really felt like home anymore. Yet another radical change in the last nine months.

"I guess you're right," Sam said, after another surreptitious look over Katrina's shoulder. "We waited too long, anyway. Looks like he's moved to another aisle."

They found the items they needed and moved to the next aisle as well, but didn't bump into Bowie again.

Maybe he had taken the boy, whoever he was, out of the store so he could cope with his meltdown in private.

They were nearly finished shopping when Sam's phone rang with the ominous tone she used to identify her mother.

She pulled the device out of her purse and glared at it. "I wish I dared to ignore her, but if I do, I'll hear about it for a week."

That was nothing, she thought. If Katrina ignored *her* mother's calls while she was in town for Wyn's wedding, Charlene would probably mount a search and rescue, which was kind of funny when she thought about it. Charlene hadn't been nearly as smothering when Kat had been living halfway around the world in primitive conditions for the last nine months. But if she dared show up late for dinner, sheer panic ensued.

"I'm at the grocery store with Kat," Samantha said, a crackly layer of irritation in her voice. "I texted you that's where I would be."

Her mother responded something Katrina couldn't hear, which made Sam roll her eyes. To others, Linda Fremont could be demanding and cranky, quick to criticize. Oddly, she had always treated Katrina with tolerance and even a measure of kindness.

"Do you absolutely need it tonight?" Samantha asked, pausing a moment to listen to her mother's answer with obvious impatience written all over her features. "Fine. Yes. I can run over. I only wish you had mentioned this earlier, when I was just hanging around for three hours doing nothing, waiting for someone to show up at the shop. I'll grab it."

She shut off her phone and shoved it back into her little dangly Coach purse that she'd bought for a steal at the Salvation Army in Boise. "I need to stop in next door at the drugstore to pick up one of my mom's prescriptions. Sorry. I know we're in a rush."

"No problem. I'll finish the shopping and check out, then we can meet each other at your car when we're done."

"Hey, I just had a great idea," Sam exclaimed. "After the shower tonight, we should totally head up to Shelter Springs and grab a drink at the Painted Moose!"

Katrina tried not to groan. The last thing she wanted to do amid her lingering jet lag was visit the local bar scene, listening to the same songs, flirting with the same losers, trying to laugh at their same old, tired jokes.

"Let's play it by ear. We might be having so much fun at the shower that we won't want to leave. Plus it's Monday night, and I doubt there will be much going on at the PM."

She didn't have the heart to tell Sam she wasn't the same girl who loved nothing more than dancing with a bunch of half-drunk cowboys—or that she had a feeling she would never be that girl again. Priorities had a way of shifting when a person wasn't looking.

Sam stuck her bottom lip out in an exaggerated pout. "Don't be such a party pooper! We've only got a month together, and I've missed you *so much*!"

Great. Like she needed more guilt in her life.

"Let's play it by ear. Go grab your mom's prescription, I'll check out and we'll head over to Julia's place. We can figure out our after-party plans, well, after the party."

She could tell by Sam's pout that she would have a hard time escaping a late night with her. Maybe she could talk her into just hanging out by the lakeshore and talking.

"Okay. I guess we'd better hurry if we want to have time to make our salad."

Sam hurried toward the front doors, and Katrina turned back to her list. Only the items from the vegetable aisle, then she would be done. She headed in that direction and spotted a flustered Bowie Callahan trying to keep the boy with him from eating grapes from the display.

"Stop it, Milo. I told you, you can eat as many as you want *after* we buy them."

This only seemed to make the boy more frustrated. She could see by his behavior and his repetitive mannerisms that he quite possibly had some sort of developmental issues. Autism, she would guess at a glance—though that could be a gross generalization, and she was not an expert, anyway.

Whatever the case, Callahan seemed wholly unprepared to deal with it. He hadn't taken the boy out of the store, obviously, to give him a break from the overstimulation. In fact, things seemed to have progressed from bad to worse.

Milo—cute name—reached for another grape despite the warning, and Bowie grabbed his hand and sternly looked down into his face. "I said, stop it. We'll have grapes after we pay for them."

The boy didn't like that. He wrenched his hand away and threw himself to the ground. "No! No! No!" he chanted.

"That's enough," Bowie Callahan snapped, loudly enough that other shoppers turned around to stare, which made the man flush.

She could see Milo was gearing up for a nuclear meltdown—and while she reminded herself it was none of her business, she couldn't escape a certain sense of professional obligation to step in.

She wanted to ignore it, to turn into the next aisle, finish her shopping and escape the store as quickly as she could. She could come up with a dozen excuses about why that was the best course of action. Samantha would be waiting for her. She didn't know the man or his frustrated kid. She had plenty of troubles of her own to worry about.

None of that held much weight when compared with the sight of a child, who clearly had some special needs, in great distress—and an adult who just as clearly didn't know what to do in the situation.

She felt an unexpected pang of sympathy for Bowie Callahan, probably because her mother had told her so many stories about how mortified Charlene would be when Katrina would have a seizure in a public place. All the staring, the pointing, the whispers.

The boy continued to chant "no" and began smacking his palm against his forehead in rhythm with each exclamation. A couple of older women she didn't know— tourists, probably—looked askance at the boy, and one muttered something to the other about how some children needed a swat on the behind.

She wanted to tell the old biddies to mind their own business but held her tongue, since she was about to ignore her own advice.

After another minute passed, when Bowie Callahan did nothing but gaze down at the boy with helpless frustration, Katrina knew she had to act. What other choice did she have? She pushed her cart closer. The man briefly met her gaze with a wariness that she chose to ignore. Instead, she plopped onto the ground next to the distressed boy.

In her experience with children of all ages and abilities, they reacted better to someone willing to lower to their level. She wasn't sure if he even noticed she was there, since he didn't stop chanting or smacking his palm against his head.

"Hi there." She spoke in a calm, conversational tone, as if she was chatting with one of her friends at Wynona's shower later in the evening. "What's your name?"

Milo—whose name she knew perfectly well from hearing Bowie use it—barely took a breath. "No! No! No! No!"

"Mine is Katrina," she went on. "Some people call me Kat. You know. Kitty-cat. Meow. Meow."

His voice hitched a little, and he lowered his hand but continued chanting, though he didn't sound quite as distressed. "No. No. No."

"Let me guess," she said. "Is your name Batman?"

He frowned. "No. No. No."

"Is it… Anakin Skywalker?"

She picked the name, assuming by his Star Wars T-shirt it would be familiar to him. He shook his head. "No."

"What about Harry Potter?

This time, he looked intrigued at the question, or perhaps at her stupidity. He shook his head.

"How about Milo?"

Big blue eyes widened with shock. "No," he said, though his tone gave the word the opposite meaning.

"Milo. Hi there. I like your name. I've never met anybody named Milo. Do you know anybody else named Kat?"

He shook his head.

"Neither do I," she admitted. "But I have a cat. Her name is Marshmallow, because she's all white. Do you like marshmallows? The kind you eat, I mean."

He nodded and she smiled. "I do, too. Especially in hot cocoa."

He pantomimed petting a cat and pointed at her.

"You'd like to pet her? She would like that. She lives with my mom now and loves to have anyone pay attention to her. Do you have a cat or a dog, Milo?"

The boy's forehead furrowed, and he shook his head, glaring up at the man beside him, who looked stonily down at both of them.

Apparently that was a touchy subject.

Did the boy talk? She had heard him say only "no" so far. It wasn't uncommon for children on the autism spectrum and with other developmental delays to have much better receptive language skills than expressive skill, and he obviously understood and could get his response across fairly well without words.

"I see lots of delicious things in your cart—including cherries. Those are my favorite. Yum. I must have missed those. Where did you find them?"

He pointed to another area of the produce section, where a gorgeous display of cherries gleamed under the fluorescent lights.

She pretended she didn't see them. Though the boy's tantrum had been averted for now, she didn't think it would hurt anything if she distracted him a little longer. "Do you think you could show me?"

It was a technique she frequently employed with her students who might be struggling, whether that was socially, emotionally or academically. She found that if she enlisted their help—either to assist her or to help out another student—they could often be distracted enough that they forgot whatever had upset them.

Milo craned his neck to look up at Bowie Callahan for permission. The man looked down at both of them, a baffled look on his features, but after a moment he shrugged and reached a hand down to help her off the floor.

She didn't need assistance, but it would probably seem rude to ignore him. She placed her hand in his and found it warm and solid and much more calloused than a computer nerd should have. She tried not to pay attention to the little shock of electricity between them or the tug at her nerves.

"Thanks," she mumbled, looking quickly away as she followed the boy, who, she was happy to notice, seemed to have completely forgotten his frustration.

Don't miss SERENITY HARBOR
by RaeAnne Thayne
available wherever HQN books and ebooks are sold!

COMING NEXT MONTH FROM

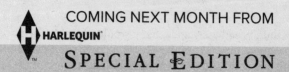

HARLEQUIN

SPECIAL EDITION

Available July 18, 2017

#2563 MOMMY AND THE MAVERICK
Montana Mavericks: The Great Family Roundup
by Meg Maxwell

Billionaire businessman Autry Jones swore off single mothers after enduring the pain of losing both the woman he loved *and* her child when she dumped him. That is, until he meets widowed mother of three Marissa Jones, who changes his mind—and his life—in three weeks.

#2564 DO YOU TAKE THIS COWBOY?
Thunder Mountain Brotherhood • by Vicki Lewis Thompson

Recently returned to Wyoming from New Zealand, Austin Teague is determined to find a wife and settle down. But he manages to fall hard for the fiercely independent Drew Martinelli, the one woman who's dead set against getting married.

#2565 HOW TO TRAIN A COWBOY
Texas Rescue • by Caro Carson

Benjamin Graham is a former marine, not a cowboy. So when he gets a job as a ranch hand, he has a lot to learn. Luckily, Emily Davis is willing to teach him everything he needs to know. But as the attraction between them grows, Graham and Emily will both have to face their pasts and learn to embrace the future.

#2566 VEGAS WEDDING, WEAVER BRIDE
Return to the Double C • by Allison Leigh

It looks like Penny Garner and Quinn Templeton had a Vegas wedding when they wake up in bed together with rings and a marriage certificate. While they put off a divorce to determine if she's pregnant, can Quinn convince Penny to leave her old heartbreak in the past and become his Weaver bride?

#2567 THE RANCHER'S UNEXPECTED FAMILY
The Cedar River Cowboys • by Helen Lacey

Helping Cole Quartermaine reconnect with his daughter was all Ash McCune intended to do. Falling for the sexy single dad was not part of the plan. But plans, she quickly discovers, have a way of changing!

#2568 AWOL BRIDE
Camden Family Secrets • by Victoria Pade

After a car accident leaves runaway bride Maicy Clark unconscious, she's rescued by the last man on earth she ever wanted to see again: Conor Madison, her high school sweetheart, who rejected her eighteen years ago. And if that isn't bad enough, she's stranded in a log cabin with him, in the middle of a raging blizzard, with nothing to do but remember just how good they were together.

YOU CAN FIND MORE INFORMATION ON UPCOMING HARLEQUIN® TITLES, FREE EXCERPTS AND MORE AT WWW.HARLEQUIN.COM.

HSECNM0717

Billionaire businessman Autry Jones swore off single mothers—until he meets widowed mom of three Marissa Jones just weeks before he's supposed to leave for a job in Paris...

Read on for a sneak preview of
MOMMY AND THE MAVERICK
by **Meg Maxwell**, *the second book in the*
MONTANA MAVERICKS: THE GREAT FAMILY
ROUNDUP continuity.

"Right. We shook on being friends. But..." She paused and dropped down onto the love seat across from the fireplace.

"But things feel more than friendly between us," he finished for her. "There was that kiss, for one. And the fact that every time I see you I want to kiss you again."

"Ditto. See the problem?"

He smiled and sat down beside her. "Marissa, why did you come here? To tell me that doing the competition with Abby is a bad idea? That she's going to get too attached to me?"

"Yup."

"Except you didn't say that."

"Because I don't want to take it from her. I want her to be excited about the competition. To not lose out on something when she's been dealt a hard blow in life so young. But yeah, I am worried she's going to get too attached. All three girls. But especially Abby."

"Abby knows I'm leaving for Paris at the end of August. That's a given. Goodbye is already in the air, Marissa. We're not fooling anyone."

"Why do I keep fighting it, then?" she asked. "Why do I have to keep reminding myself that feeling the way I do about you is only going to—"

"Make you feel like crap when I go? I know. I've had that same talk with myself fifty times. I wasn't expecting to meet you, Marissa. Or want you so damned bad every time I see you."

It wasn't just about sex, but he wasn't putting that out there. If she kept it to sexual attraction, surface stuff, maybe he'd believe it. Then he could enjoy his time with Marissa and go in a couple weeks without much strain in his chest.

"So what do we do?" she asked. "Give in to this or be smart and stay nice and platonic?"

He reached for her hand. "I don't know."

"Your hair's still damp," she said. "I can smell your shampoo. And your soap."

He leaned closer and kissed her, his hands slipping around her shoulders, down her back, drawing her to him. He felt her stiffen for a second and then relax. "I don't want to just be friends, Marissa. I want you."

She kissed him back, her hands in his hair, and he could feel her breasts against his chest. He sucked in a breath, overwhelmed by desire, by need. "You're sure?" he asked, pulling back a bit to look at her, directly into her beautiful dark brown eyes.

"No, I'm not sure," she whispered. "I just know that I want you, too."

Don't miss
MOMMY AND THE MAVERICK by Meg Maxwell,
available August 2017 wherever
Harlequin® Special Edition books and ebooks are sold.

www.Harlequin.com

Reward the book lover in you!

Earn points from all your Harlequin book purchases from wherever you shop.

Turn your points into *FREE BOOKS* of your choice
OR
EXCLUSIVE GIFTS from your favorite authors or series.

Join for FREE today at
www.HarlequinMyRewards.com.

Harlequin My Rewards is a free program (no fees) without any commitments or obligations.

MYR17